THE SEQUEL TO *COMING HOME*

TO DO
THE RIGHT
THING

A NOVEL

Edward K. Mackendrik

THE SEQUEL TO *COMING HOME*

TO DO
THE RIGHT
THING

A NOVEL

Edward K. Mackendrik

IMPERIUM PUBLISHING
CREATE YOUR STORY

CHAPTER 2

It was early when Arnold heard a knock on the ranch house door. He moved quickly across the small house to answer it.

Standing on the porch was Jerry Walker a local ranch hand and horseman who had been hired to help Beth when Arnold returned to Oklahoma. Jerry was a wiry man, shorter by a head than Arnold, slender, but strong. His reddish blonde hair curled out from under the brim of his battered cowboy hat. His smile was friendly and open. Beth had told Arnold how happy she was with Jerry's work, and Arnold saw as soon as he had inspected the ranch that Jerry was making good progress repairing the fences.

"Mornin' Arnold," Jerry said. "I've a morning surprise for you." He pointed to the corral where a baby calf stood near the fence. Its mother came into view from around the barn, crying as she walked up to the calf, wanting to ensure her calf was okay. With the reunion of baby and mother, every-thing was fine.

"Good Morning Jerry. Looks like someone is early and I don't mean you. I just checked the calendar and was thinking that we would begin to see new calves in three weeks," Arnold laughed.

Arnold and Jerry walked out to the barn to get a closer look at the new calf. As he approached, Arnold noticed Black Shadow start pacing, demonstrating his need for attention. Arnold walked up to the stallion and gave him a big hug over the fence and talked to him as though he was a member of his family.

"Look here Big Guy, a new calf for us to watch over." Black Shadow nudged Arnold in the chest as he usually did.

Jerry and Arnold swung up on the fence, sitting on the top board, studying the new calf and mother. Both looked healthy. Arnold thought about how much Beth would enjoy hearing the news. He would be picking her up first thing this morning at the hospital to bring her home. Jerry headed back out onto the range to look for more new calves while Arnold headed to Pueblo to pick up Beth.

An hour later, Arnold walked into Beth Houser's room at the Mountain View Hospital in Pueblo, Colorado. He found Beth sitting up in her chair, dressed, and ready to go home. Her long brown hair was brushed and pulled back in a ponytail. She smiled happily at Arnold.

"Hi. Thank you for coming to get me," Beth said, "I am so ready to go home."

"You look ready to go home. Are you feeling okay?" Arnold asked.

Beth nodded. "I have some pain pills for the pain from the incisions until they heal. I'll have to build up my strength a bit though."

While a nurse came into the room and had Beth sign some papers, Arnold found a spare wheelchair and brought it back to the room for Beth. She stood up carefully and moved over to the wheelchair.

"Thank you for your care." Beth said to the nurse.

"You are welcome sweety." The nurse smiled and waved as they move down the hallway to the doors to the parking lot.

"I can't wait to see the new baby calf," Beth said as Arnold pulled the truck out of the parking lot and turned it toward Alamosa.

"You will love the little devil."

"What is Alice like?"

"Sweet as Shoo Ann."

"That is wonderful," Beth sighed.

After a few miles of driving in silence, Arnold looked over to see that Beth had laid her head on the door frame and was asleep. She looked a little pale to him, but he was sure she would improve quickly at home.

When they got to Beth Ranch, Arnold went around the truck and woke Beth gently. He gathered her up in his arms and carried her into the ranch house where he laid her on her bed. She smiled sleepily.

"So glad to be home," she murmured.

Arnold went back out and got what luggage she had and set it in her room.

Beth slept for several hours. When she woke up, she was alert and hungry. Shoo Ann brought her food from the restaurant and helped her walk out to the kitchen so she could eat with company.

Jerry and Arnold were eating their lunches at the kitchen table discussing rounding up the expectant cows. Since deliveries had started, their plan was to drive them from the far pastures to the pasture near the house.

"They can return to the farther pastures once the mother and calf are healthy and the calf castrated and vaccinated." Arnold was saying.

Jerry nodded in agreement over the rim of his coffee cup.

Beth, who was listening asked, "Why are you proceeding in this way? I have not done any of that in years past."

"We want to take this precautionary step to reduce the number of calves that die mysteriously," Arnold answered.

"Can I watch a cow deliver?" Shoo Ann asked. "I've never seen such a thing."

"Sure. You can help deliver any of the calves that the mother cannot deliver on her own," Arnold said.

"What would be expected of me?" she asked.

"You will need to grab hold of the baby's front legs when they appear in the birth canal and pull hard, very hard, and continue to do so until the baby comes out."

"It can be a bloody and muddy process," Jerry added.

Shoo Ann thought about it. Then said, "I guess I will do what I can do."

The two men left Shoo Ann and Beth to finish their meal and headed out to their horses.

It took several hours to find the individual cows and maneuver them into a herd. As the cows approached the corral, Arnold pointed out several cows that were acting strangely. Jerry recognized the behavior.

"They're about to deliver," he shouted.

They hustled all the cows into the corral and watched several of the cows deliver calves right then. Jerry and Arnold discussed the vaccinations. They planned to vaccinate in 3 weeks, and they agreed to put an ear tag in each of the calf's left ear for identification and counting purposes when they had them in the vaccination chute. For now, they would rely on the fact that the mothers knew their calves to keep them straight.

Shoo Ann helped deliver a calf later that evening.

She came into the ranch house where Beth was resting, mud from head to foot and stripped off her boots and all her clothes at the door. In her damp underwear, she washed her arms and face at the kitchen sink and then ran to her room and stuck her head around the door as she dressed in dry clothes.

"Beth. I had to get really close to the back end of the mama cow. There, I saw two little hooves sticking out a hole under the cow's tail, and I grabbed them and pulled and pulled. "The slippery thing came out finally. The baby was long and as big as I am. It knocked me over in the mud. Landed right on top of me. Covered me with slime. I had to wrestle the baby calf off me so Arnold and I could rub it down so it would start breathing. It was amazing. After that, the mama cow took over and licked the calf until it stood up."

Beth laughed. "I've seen a calf born, but never that close up."

Over the next three days, all 200 impregnated cows gave birth. There were now 200 healthy calves. Seventy-five of the calves were male and 125 heifers. Arnold and Jerry separated the cows with male calves from the others so they could castrate the males as soon as possible. Arnold contacted the veterinarian to castrate the calves because he did not want to make a mistake by doing it himself. The veterinarian showed up each day and castrated any new male calves that were born that day until all the cows had delivered their calves.

Beth came out with Shoo Ann the next day to watch the castration of the bull calves. Shoo Ann watched the castrations with discomfort. She did not like that the calves were losing their ability to reproduce.

At the end of the week, Arnold and Jerry opened the gate to the corral and let the cows and calves go back onto the larger ranch pasture where the calves would gain weight. One day, they would be sold. As they watched the main herd move slowly out of the corral, they discussed the 30 calves purchased in the early spring and decided they were ready to sell. Arnold contacted the Auction House, and they agreed to pick them up in three days. Jerry and he decided to begin the roundup of those 30 calves the next day. Shoo Ann wanted to assist, and they welcomed her to their party.

When the roundup of the 30 calves was complete, Arnold relaxed on a bale of hay next to Black Shadow in the barn. Everyone else had left. After the busy day and in the quiet barn, he began to recount the experiences he had encountered since leaving Oklahoma on July 7, 1956, over a year ago. He realized the journey had done wonders for him. He no longer felt injured by the horrible experiences surrounding his divorce. The whole mess had clarified in his mind, and he had apparently put it behind him. The divorce and betrayal of his wife no longer dominated his thinking, and he hardly ever thought about it.

Working with the castrated calves reminded Arnold of the time he had spent with Brenda and her father, Henry Gladstone doctoring castrated calves on Henry's ranch in New Mexico. Henry had died a year ago. Arnold had helped Brenda sell their ranch, and she had stayed in Denver where Henry had died. Arnold still called her to see if she was okay and ready to move on.

Brenda was beautiful, and Arnold was pretty sure he was in love with her still. When Arnold met Brenda, she had been a virgin, a forward virgin, but truly innocent, nevertheless. When Arnold first met her, Brenda was keeping house for her elderly father on their New Mexico ranch. She helped with the cattle too and sometimes rode out with Arnold to help him with his ranch chores and to spend time near him. She had never been far beyond the ranch boundaries in her life. She had not known many men other than her father either. On her very first vacation, in Santa Fe, one arranged by Arnold for the three of them, she had eagerly accepted Arnold as her first lover. In his mind's eye, he could still see her smiling at him, always smiling; whether tall in the saddle or stretched out on white sheets, she smiled, her red gold hair swirling about her face as she turned to laugh at him.

Arnold fell in love with Brenda. For reasons he could not understand, she stayed in Denver after her father's death receiving comfort from the company of a chaplain that had been there when Henry died. Arnold was jealous of the chaplain, and Brenda and he fought over her attachment to him. Arnold was sure it was sexual, but Brenda refused to discuss it. Even now when he called her, she refused to tell him what he wanted to know, "was she sleeping with the Chaplain?" In the end his pride and his conviction that she was betraying him drove him away.

He still called her. She still saw the Chaplain. She was still silent about the nature of the relationship. Until that changed, Arnold would torture himself with jealousy and could not let her back into his life

With some effort, Arnold pushed away thoughts of Brenda and thought instead about the cheerier subject of the income he was receiving from his gas and oil wells in Oklahoma. Mostly, in quiet time like this, he spent his time thinking about how to use his God-given assets to help people who were less fortunate. Beth was one of them. He had decided to do his best to keep Beth pleased with her life. Her life certainly had been a precious bucket of pits prior to their becoming acquainted.

Edward K. Mackendrik

CHAPTER 3

It is Saturday, Arnold thought as he finished his first cup of coffee in the kitchen at the Beth Ranch. The September sun was already making it warm outside.

Arnold decided to find the gelding that Beth had ridden before she got Autumn Time and bring him to the barn. This took longer than he anticipated because the horse was on the far side of the pasture and had not been ridden lately. Arnold had to walk out, catch him, and lead him back to the barn. Arnold's thinking was to prepare him for Alice and Shoo Ann to ride with Arnold along on Black Shadow. It was apparent the horse did not like the stallion, but Arnold put him in the corral with feed and water and anticipated putting a saddle on him later in the day.

Shoo Ann and Alice drove Beth's pickup from the motel to the ranch and met Arnold at the barn. Arnold had seen Alice before at the restaurant. He knew she was a couple of years older than Shoo Ann. As he looked her over now, he wondered if she was a virgin. He doubted it.

Alice's first horse lesson began with learning to saddle. She watched Arnold saddle Black Stallion and then helped Shoo Ann saddle Autumn Time. Shoo Ann taught her how to get up into the saddle and how to dismount. Shoo Ann wanted Alice to ride double with Arnold before attempting to ride on her own. So, Arnold mounted and reached down to help Alice mount in front of him.

Even with her slender body, the saddle was cramped with Alice and Arnold in it. Trying to concentrate on giving a horseback riding lesson, Arnold first explained the different gaits a horse walked or ran at and then showed Alice how to "steer" the horse with the reins. He let her guide Black Shadow with the reins for a mile or so while he sat back with his hands resting on her hips. Soon, the feel of her butt rubbing his crotch was making it difficult for Arnold to concentrate on giving riding instructions. He also noticed Alice continued to scoot back and make a lot of contact.

After about an hour of riding, Alice moved his hands down, so they were firmly in contact with her crotch. He allowed his fingers to explore, press, and rub along the seam of her jeans. She smiled at him over her shoulder and breathing faster, whispered,

"Maybe we could gallop?"

The gallop lasted for only a few minutes before the two had to concentrate on staying in the saddle. Alice felt warm and moist beneath his fingers even through her jeans and his erection was pressed hard into her back. He slid her zipper down as they slowed to a walk. His large fingers pushed the fabric of her panties aside and slid down into the heat of her passage. She cried out and pumped her body frantically on his finger. His other hand moved up to press into her breast. She came with a silent intensity that tightened her whole body into an arch, like a bow; and unconsciously, she stood up in the stirrups.

Arnold pulled her tight jeans down past her knees then pulled her into his lap so he could pull her boots and jeans off all the way. He discarded the clothing and turned her to face him. He set her down straddling his lap. He unzipped his own jeans and released his hard penis. Pushing aside the flimsy fabric of her panties, he entered her and pressing on her hip bones, he pulled her down tight on him. Alice's bare feet found purchase on his boots in the stirrups and she was able to leverage herself up and down on him. Arnold pressed her harder and harder onto him and soon Alice climaxed a second time, the tremors of her body bringing him to climax with her.

For a while, they sat atop Black Shadow wrapped together, exhausted and uncaring that they were exposed in an open meadow. Alice held tight to Arnold's neck and her bare legs hung over Arnold's jeaned thighs. Arnold left himself buried in Alice's warmth for several minutes. Then, he lifted her up and carefully helped her slide down to the ground. He zipped up his jeans and dismounted. She stood before him in her short-sleeved shirt, panties, and bare feet. She giggled, making him smile.

"I guess we had better find your pants and boots," he chuckled.

Alice guffawed. She spun around in a circle, uncertain from which direction they had come.

Arnold spotted the clothing not too far away and swung Alice up in his arms and carried her to her pants and boots. He watched as she dressed.

They remounted Black Shadow and walked the stallion to Arnold's favorite spot along the bubbling spring and little stream among the trees. They stopped and pulling a blanket out of the saddlebag, they sat down to rest and get acquainted.

Arnold thought that Alice was exciting to talk and listen to. She spoke English very well. Like her sister Shoo Ann, Alice was eager to learn about everything. Arnold allowed Alice to walk Black Shadow slowly doing practice turns and halts so she could become more familiar with horses. She seemed to be thrilled by the horse.

"Arnold. When can I have my own pony?"

"I've already got an extra pony you can ride whenever you want when you have had some more training," Arnold said. "I'll show him to you when we get back to the ranch."

The two headed back to the ranch hungry for lunch. At the barn, Shoo Ann waited. Arnold showed them the gelding that Beth had ridden before she got Autumn Time.

"Shoo Ann is used to riding Autumn Time," Arnold stated. "This one, whose name I do not know can be the horse you ride, Alice."

Shoo Ann and Alice exchanged wide grins.

"Thank you so much. Arnold." Alice said and wrapped her arms around him at waist level. "I am so glad we fit so well in the saddle together," she murmured into his shirt.

An hour later, Beth, on the mend after her surgery, was up and around more and found Arnold in the barn lounging on the bale of hay.

"There you are," she said. "I wanted to discuss something with you."

"We can go back to the house," Arnold suggested, "and be more comfortable while we talk."

They walked slowly back to the house, Arnold measuring his pace to Beth's.

Once Beth was settled on the couch and Arnold had a tumbler of ice and bourbon beside him, he asked, "What did you want to talk about?"

"I have been talking to, or should I say the Banker in Alamosa has been talking to me, and he has stirred my interest more than just a little bit. His name is David Baker. He told me he had been discussing an important project with the nuns who currently operate the sanctuary near Alamosa that houses young homeless girls. Currently there are 15 girls living in the house, all under the age of 18, and the city has condemned the building. The nuns are going to be forced to close their shelter and demolish the building because it is unsafe."

"Mr. Baker has proposed that I sell the 5 acres of land adjacent to the highway to a trust owner for the purpose of building and operating a sanctuary for these children and others that may need to live there. He wants to start a charitable organization that would then own and operate the sanctuary for the benefit of the children and the nuns. This charitable organization would be responsible for administering the donations, paying the bills, and supervising the raising of the children that live there until they are 18 years old and capable of taking care of themselves. Now, I want to know what you think of this idea."

Arnold sat completely startled by the proposal and needed to ask questions he thought Beth could not answer, but he knew he had to begin somewhere. So, he asked, "Beth, how much do you want for the 5 acres?"

Beth said, "$300.00."

"Okay, assuming they buy it, how are they going to make all the improvements to your property, such as water, sewer, gas and electricity? All of these must go through your ranch. Are you going to provide them a right-of-way easement so this can be accomplished and if so, how much are you going to charge them for the easement?"

Beth looked at him with a blank stare and said, "Arnold, I do not know. You tell me. This is why I asked you, you know about these things, and I don't."

Arnold genuinely thought this was a charitable organization he could support. God had allowed him to make large sums of money and he wanted the money to be used for good purposes. He already supported several charitable projects and the people who oversaw them.

Arnold assured Beth, "If you want to donate 5 to 10 acres for the purpose of building a place for children who do not have a home, I support it. I'd enjoy discussing this with the banker too if you want me to."

Beth was exuberant in her happiness and started shrieking and yelling. She grabbed him playfully and seemed to want to wrestle. Arnold laughed.

"Beth remember your stitches. Take it easy."

"I want to go immediately and tell Mr. Baker," she confessed. He agreed so she called for an appointment. The banker said they could come at once to his office and discuss specific plans.

When they arrived in Alamosa, three of the nuns were already present in the bank's conference room. Mr. Baker introduced Sister Theresa, Sister Mary Joseph, and Sister Mary Frances to Beth and Arnold.

First, they all discussed the entire concept.

"We are committed to living in the building, managing it, and taking care of the girls," stated Sister Mary Joseph.

When they began discussing more of the details, it became clear to Arnold that no one had any idea of what the cost would be. So, he helped them estimate the cost. He thought it would cost more than twenty million dollars. The nuns agreed to pursue a fund-raising effort to pay for everything. Unfortunately, it would take about 10 years to raise the five million dollars needed to purchase the land and initiate construction.

When this fact surfaced, Arnold offered, provided confidentiality could be assured, to fund the initial cost and then support the fund-raising effort. He would underwrite the remaining cost up to twenty million dollars to insure they acted promptly and with purpose.

The banker and nuns were almost as excited and gleeful as Beth. They proceeded to schedule a meeting with a reputable construction firm to obtain realistic cost estimates and discuss the start of construction.

When the construction meeting occurred, the following week, Mr. Baker, the three sisters, Beth and Arnold attended along with a representative from the City of Alamosa and the County to decide legal jurisdiction and zoning requirements. The original two-hour meeting lasted 4 hours and much was accomplished.

It was agreed that the building would accommodate up to twenty girls that would live in, six live-in nuns, class rooms for teaching students, a sanctuary for religious services, a small clinic, and public areas to house any other employees assigned to handle administration and maintenance. The design of the complex was to begin immediately, however the amount of land needed for such a building, including a landscaped area around it would require 10 acres. Beth agreed to donate the 10 acres provided she could designate the location.

Arnold established an account at the bank dedicated to the project. He knew this was needed but cautioned David Baker again to always guard against identifying him as being involved in any way. The banker agreed to this, and Arnold informed him that he would transfer electronically four deposits each totaling 5 million dollars to the new account. He asked about how he was going to ensure protection until it was used. Baker replied that he had already discussed this with an insurance company that would write the policy and have it ready within two weeks. Arnold informed him he would make the transfer after he was notified of the account number and had reviewed the insurance policy providing coverage.

Baker agreed to manage the construction project including initiating a fund raiser to facilitate public involvement and enthusiastic participation by the local Catholic church and the nun's mother house. Baker informed the group that his administrative personnel had prepared a public announcement of the project to be released when the legal paperwork was prepared and signed.

Arnold asked Baker when the construction company would begin actual work. The banker replied that the construction company had already submitted draft documents and drawings and was waiting for Beth and him to approve the drawings and/or make changes.

Everyone felt very good about their meeting and was pleased about the progress of the project when they adjourned.

On their way to the ranch Beth commented, "I have often dreamed of supporting girls who were having a difficult time with life issues. Now,

I am really doing something. Let's drive to the place I have pictured for this building. I'd like to know your opinion of the spot."

They drove along the perimeter of the ranch until Beth said, "This is it. Stop here!"

"I think this location is perfect, Beth," Arnold said as he surveyed the land.

CHAPTER 4

Arnold decided to visit Janell's ranch and ask her how things were going with her two mares. Black Shadow had serviced the mares the year before. The first time he had serviced them, the mares had come back into heat. The second time, Janell had insisted that Arnold bring Black Shadow to her ranch so her mares would be more responsive. Arnold did not buy her rationale but had agreed to bring Black Shadow to her ranch to humor her. It only took him about 20 minutes to ride Black Shadow to her ranch. The horses had mated vigorously this second time, and he and Janell had enjoyed their own mating under an apple tree near the corral, no doubt inspired by the horses' performance.

As he drove his pick-up into the ranch yard, he found Janell herself walking from the house to the barn at that very moment. She was a tall woman, older than Beth and perhaps older than himself, but her long hair was black as night without a streaked with grey. When she heard what he was there for, she was pleased that he was concerned with her mares. As it turned out, this time, they were both pregnant.

Arnold asked Janell, "if she wanted to sell one of her mares."

"As long as I get the right price," She said. Who is doing the buying?"

"I am thinking about it." Arnold said.

"Please tell me what you think is a good price for the black one with the white face?" Janell asked. "She is a four-year old, has been bred one time and is due to have a little one in four months. What are you planning to do with her? You already have Black Shadow?"

I need to provide a pony for a friend. Will you accept "$300.00 for the mare?"

"I will take that," Janell said.

They agreed and shook hands. Arnold paid her for the mare and told Janell he would return for her the next day.

"You are of course welcome any time."

Returning to the Beth Ranch, Arnold told Beth about his purchase. She decided to head for the restaurant and find Alice.

"Alice," she called as soon as she opened the door and saw the young woman serving in the dining room. "You are the proud owner of a mare and you can begin riding her as soon as you get a saddle and all the supporting riding gear."

Alice's smile was so bright it lit up the little dining room.

"Who should I thank?" she asked.

Beth replied, "Arnold performed the good deed."

"I will find some way to thank him," Alice promised. "How much does a saddle and gear cost?'

"About $50.00 if you are not too picky about the saddle. Some saddles cost more than a thousand dollars," Beth warned.

"$50.00 sounds best, but I might not want to spend all of that at one time because I will then be flat broke until pay day," Alice sighed.

"Don't worry. Arnold plans to take you shopping tomorrow after you and he pick up the mare. I know you will want to go along on that excursion."

After delivering the happy news to Alice, Beth returned to the ranch feeling pleased with herself and with Arnold. Arnold, she found, had decided to go to bed early because he was tired after an active day that had started very early in the morning. Beth decided that it was time for her to retire also and she went into their bedroom and laid down beside him. She undressed and moved close to him.

"Maybe I can help you relax and sleep," she whispered. Arnold smiled wide without opening his eyes. He knew she was very good at her relaxation techniques.

Beth ran her hands all over his shoulders, chest, hips and thighs, sometimes massaging and sometimes using such a light touch it tickled. Very deliberately, she avoided his pubic area and the center of his desire that rose up there. She nibbled here and there and then took him into her mouth and gently sucked. Arnold let a harsh breath out. He reached for her hair and had to remind himself to gentle his grasp as he climaxed almost immediately under the touch of her tongue.

Beth threw her arm over Arnold and the two slept soundly until the early morning. She woke first and informed Arnold she had to leave to drive to a meeting with the Catholic nuns and city representatives. He mumbled, acknowledging that he had heard and went back to sleep.

Later that morning, Alice, Shoo Ann and Arnold headed out in the pickup with Arnold's horse trailer on behind to purchase a saddle, a bridle, two blankets and saddle bags for Alice at the same store where Shoo Ann had bought her riding equipment. Alice was very anxious to have everything ready when her new pony arrived. Arnold said he understood.

All the way to the Janell ranch, where they would pick up Alice's pony, Arnold was entertained listening to Alice and Shoo Ann talk about their plans when Alice could go riding with her.

Janell greeted them and helped them load the black and white mare into the trailer. Alice was instantly in love with her pony and happy that she would get to pick a name for her. As he had with Shoo Ann, Arnold suggested she wait a few days to let her experiences with the horse give her clues to the most appropriate name for the mare. As soon as they arrived back at the Beth Ranch, Alice and Shoo Ann led the mare to the barn and put Alice's new saddle and gear on the horse. They saddled Shoo Ann's horse too and rode out of the barn to practice walking and steering.

Arnold retired to the porch with a cup of coffee and watched the Alice and Shoo Ann ride out through the pasture. He could not stop himself from thinking of Oklahoma. He decided he needed to write a plan and determine if it would work. He retrieved a notebook and pen from inside the ranch house and settled in to think and write. He could not think of a single plan to write about that sounded workable. Soon he gave up and went into the house and fell asleep with the radio on, He was awakened by Shoo Ann and Alice.

"Arnold. Can we play?" they asked staring down at him, one on each side of the bed.

Arnold mumbled an assent.

They smiled happily down at him as they undressed him and then themselves, exposing their small breasts and narrow waists and hips to his view. They were delicate in build and in color. Their nipples were pink and the tiny triangles of pubic hair that crowned the meeting of their thighs were dark and neatly trimmed.

They seemed to dive onto him, like mermaids, sliding over his skin, bringing his hands to their skin in invitation. He definitely explored everywhere he could reach.

After a while he was not sure which Asian lady was inside him or which he was inside. They probed every niche and entry to his body and opened theirs's to him. All was smoothness and heat until one than the other lady climaxed in a powerful tensing of lean muscles that dragged him along behind them into oblivion. When he woke, he was entangled in smooth limbs and tiny hands grasped his large body.

"Ah Arnold," Shoo Ann whispered, "You are so large, it takes two of us to hold you. Two of us to surround you. And, two times to satisfy you."

With that she flipped over on top of him and took his hardening penis inside herself and rocked as if she was riding her mare. He grew instantly bigger. Alice lay to his side and lazily stroke both him and her sister where they joined, seemingly intrigued by the physical connection of their bodies. Her fingers played over them. She explored their nipples and elbows, and belly buttons as they mated. Everything was a lot slower this time and Shoo Ann climax first when Arnold put his finger on the hard, little nub that hid within her pubic patch. Arnold followed as his body responded to Alice's tempting touches and Shoo Ann's body demanding satisfaction.

Arnold could not remember ever having an experience such as this, with two Asian ladies, exploring new ways to enjoy each other and him.

When Beth returned from her meeting in Pueblo, Arnold he asked to discuss a private matter with her.

"What are your thoughts regarding your enjoyment of both Shoo Ann in a lesbian relationship and me in a heterosexual relationship?"

Beth said, "It is quite simple. I enjoy both of you. I have enjoyed Shoo Ann for a long time; and more recently, I have enjoyed both you and Shoo Ann."

She continued saying, "I do not see a problem with it from my own moral perspective since I am not harming anyone. Everyone involved is aware of the other party, and it seems no one has a problem with it."

Then she asked, "Do you object to me making love to Shoo Ann and then making love to you?"

Before Arnold could reply, Beth said "If you do not object, we have no problem."

Arnold said, "I do not have a problem with it as long as it is Shoo Ann. If it expands to others, I will object in a serious way. I cannot accept the practice if it is with anyone else."

"Then we do not have a problem."

Arnold agreed and decided to not worry about it.

Arnold poured himself a whiskey over ice and sauntered out to the hay barn, planning his next trip to Oklahoma.

He continued to be haunted by nostalgia for his home in Oklahoma. He yearned to be there, to walk across the farm and dream of the life he lived long ago and the one he hoped to live there again.

He was not dissatisfied with his travel and his purpose to find new adventures and meet new people who were good people yet different. His strategy appeared to be working. He recognized that he was more content now than before he started traveling. He accepted his improved happiness for longer periods of time as proof that he should continue traveling. He decided, when needed, to travel back to Oklahoma to satisfy his longing for home.

When he thought of meeting good and different people, his mind naturally turned first to Brenda and then to Beth. Beth was an intersex person. The goodness of her person was obvious in her sense of fairness and in her loving of others and in her desire to live a simple life. He accepted all of this without question.

He asked himself, Why look further for a mate when Beth satisfied his sexual needs and exhibited other qualities that are seldom found in a relationship, such as trust, honesty and a demonstrated willingness to share anything and everything she owned with him?

The question 'why not marriage?' always bothers me, he admitted to himself. The answer has not yet occurred to me, so I continue to search for it. I believe the answer will come to me in time.

Arnold settled back in the hay loft and continued to give himself a pep talk and to build a plan.

He decided to make plans to travel to Oklahoma for more than a short stay before winter set in. He wanted to walk across the farm and dream. Then, he would think of the future and decide how to proceed while continuing to listen to his own feelings. He wanted to be sure to make plans that incorporated what he remembered from childhood with what he remembered of young adulthood with the past experiences of adulthood and his current situation.

"Be honest with yourself in every situation and do not avoid reality, moral values, desires, your conscience, or your learned experiences," he thought.

Arnold wanted his trip to Oklahoma to be unhurried and not obsessed with business this time. He wanted to adopt a new way of life. He wanted to allow leisure to creep into his life creating enjoyment and relaxation. He decided to schedule a round trip on an airline with an open return date.

Towards evening, Arnold drifted back to the ranch house. He used the phone there to schedule a departure date one week away. He told Beth about his plan and explained to her that he would return after he concluded his business in Oklahoma. Beth did not understand the open ticket, and it began to concern her that she would not know when or if he would return. Arnold tried to reassure her, but the ticket continued to worry Beth. So, to put a stop to this unnecessary concern, Arnold changed the return date to one month after the departure date.

Beth was not satisfied with this either and asked to go with him because she did not want the two of them to be separated for such a long period of time. He changed the return date to two weeks. Beth was happy and so was Arnold.

Going to bed that night, with Arnold planning to depart the next morning, Beth became extremely affectionate. She kissed Arnold many times. It appeared Beth had an insatiable appetite for expressing her love for him. By morning, if Beth was trying to convince him of her love for him, she had succeeded. All night long she woke him and loved him in new ways. He was sure he had never before been treated as Beth treated him. Well into the next day, he was still remembering and replaying the many things she did to him.

Sometime during that night, Beth asked him, "Why have you never expressed a desire to have children?"

He told her, "I am not certain I want children. My parents had both good and horrible experiences with their large family. Three of their thirteen children died prematurely, and one adopted son died when he was a young man. I do not believe I can live through the loss of a daughter or son. My parents shared their thoughts with me sometimes and they were almost unbearable. I witnessed both my father and mother go through the grieving process. It was terrible. I decided that I will never put myself in a position to experience losing a child. Perhaps I will change my mind, someday, but for now, I will avoid that possibility of pain."

"Is adoption acceptable to you?" Beth asked.

"No. I would love an adopted daughter or son with the same intensity as a child born to us, so there is no difference," Arnold stated.

There was silence for a while, and both looked at the ceiling.

"Beth," Arnold spoke to the ceiling, "for now let us enjoy the times we can have with each other and not plan an offspring."

Beth rose on her elbow and looked down into his face in the partial darkness. "Ok."

CHAPTER 5

Arnold departed for Oklahoma on a TWA flight serving fresh brewed coffee just the way he liked it. He had given himself a two-week window in which to think about whether he should return to Oklahoma permanently. He purposely did not inform anyone on the Oklahoma end that he was arriving. He wanted the freedom to conduct his business without interruption and to spend his free time and his time for relaxation with those he chose spontaneously.

His rental car was waiting for him, and he drove to the El Reno motel, a two-story motor court constructed of brick and metal on the outskirts of the town of El Reno.

He entered the lobby and asked the plump middle-aged redhead behind the desk to rent a room for one week.

"Ah can rent ya the same room fer two weeks at jest one half the reg'lar price if ya want," she offered giving him a bright welcoming smile.

"I'll pass for now," Arnold said. "I might be able to earn the second week before the end of the first week."

The attendant looked at him curiously. "Ah di'n't get all of what ya said."

"I think if you were interested, you would have heard me," Arnold answered.

Still not understanding, looking at him as if he were speaking a foreign language, but still smiling she said, "Wahl, Ah did hear ya, Ah jest di'n't understand ya. Ya have a nice day now."

Arnold departed for a café where he bought some coffee. After that, his first stop was to see Darrell at the bank and get an update on the balance of his account.

"Howdy Arnold. Good to see you." Darrell greeted him with an outstretched hand coming out from behind the polished bank counter. Arnold took his hand and shook it warmly. Darrell had been his banker for many years. The two men had gone to school together, become interested in money and investing and had grown into a successful money-making team. Darrell was blonde and lanky and half a foot shorter than Arnold. In a nod to his career status, he wore a leather western coat over a white shirt, string tie, and pressed jeans. He also wore dusty, unpolished cowboy boots.

"I'm just here for an update on my account, Darrell," Arnold said.

"It is going very well, Darrell said. "The income from the wells has been increasing each month, and the current plan to transfer any balance to the investment account managed by Linda is working well too. At last count, I have transferred more than 3 million to the investment account."

"I might be changing that process later, but for now everything seems to be working as intended," Arnold said. "I'll let you know if Linda, or her boss Robert, have a different accounting of the amount transferred into their hands."

Darrell asked, "What are you living on?"

"What do you mean?" Arnold asked.

"I have never seen you make a withdrawal, except for the one I received for your pick-up. Other than that, I think maybe you are living on love or the lack of it."

"I am living okay. Someday, I'll want or need to establish an account for daily withdrawals, but for now I want to save my pennies for a rainy day." Arnold said with a smile.

They both chuckled. Arnold was preparing to leave the bank to visit with Robert and Linda, his investment consultants when Darrell suggested, "While you are here, why don't we have a discussion with Betty regarding the 4H clubs and their progress?"

"I can meet here at 5:00 PM," Arnold suggested. "That way the meeting won't interfere with Betty's commitment at the school district."

"I'll coordinate with Betty," Darrell said.

Arnold arrived back at the bank promptly at 5:00 PM. Betty arrived shortly after that. She was as attractive as he remembered, smiling and tanned. She and Arnold hugged as she entered the meeting room. He and she were intimately acquainted. They were both original Okies and both single. She had lost her husband in a tractor accident years before, and she and Arnold had struck up a relationship the very first time they met to discuss the 4H projects Arnold was funding.

Today's meeting was informative and encouraging. Betty explained that there was the possibility of aiding 15 girl in the 4H program who were showing 15 head of beef (steers) and entering over 30 competitions. She reported that Arnold's land and project manager, Charlie Anderson, had been very supportive, always encouraging the girls to take care of their animals and researching better ways to feed the cows to achieve specified weight gains while keeping the animal healthy and drug free. Charlie had offered a $100.00 prize for every girl who achieved her targeted weight goal. Betty let Darrell and Arnold know that she was thrilled with the entire program.

As the meeting ended, Betty invited Arnold to her home for a home-cooked meal. Arnold accepted. He immediately began anticipating what would be served for dessert. He excused himself for a moment and phoned Linda to set up an appointment for the next day. He wanted to discuss with them his investment account activity.

Arnold followed Betty to her duplex for dinner. As soon as she opened the door, her words after the last time they made love came back to him, "You are big and hard, male, and bristly," she had murmured in his arms. "It is hard for a plain Okie woman to restrain herself with you inside her." Remembering her satisfaction was arousing.

Betty ushered him in and headed for the kitchen. He followed her and watched as she opened a bottle of red wine.

"Is meat loaf, mashed potatoes and pears all right for dinner? I have that made."

Arnold moved in close beside her. "I think we need to plan that for later." Arnold said gruffly. "Don't you?"

"Much later," Betty agreed looking at him over her wine glass. She set aside her wine and began to unbutton her blouse. Although she had had Arnold's attention before, it sharpened and focused instantly on her hands.

Very deliberately, Arnold set down his wine. He continued to watch as she shrugged her blouse off her shoulders, revealing her bra. Her arms behind her, she went to work undoing the hooks.

Betty watched Arnold watch her. She let her bra slide down her arms, revealing her large pale breasts and raspberry colored nipples. Arnold's eyes moved over her. Her shoulders and arms were tanned from working outside, but her breasts, waist and ribcage were creamy white and soft. He raised both his hands to cradle the weight of her breasts.

Her breath came faster at the first touch. He ran his fingers over her nipples watching them crinkle and harden into nubs. He continued to stroke them as she reached down to unbutton her jeans. Without interrupting the contact of her breasts with the rough, warmth of Arnold's palms, she managed to step out of her jeans and kick her shoes off.

Arnold moved both his hands to her waist and then slid the right one between her thighs, cupping her womanhood through her plain cotton panties. She was moist. He removed that hand and together his hands pulled down the elastic waist of her panties, moving them down her legs until at her knees they slid unhindered to the floor. She stepped out of them and moved into him.

Arnold replaced his hand between her legs and fingered the folds he found there. She made more room for him, parting her thighs. She began to quiver as his long middle finger stroked around the entrance to her vagina.

Arnold moved his eyes to her eyes then, withdrew his hand only long enough to unzip his jeans and released his swelling penis. He hefted her buttock up on the kitchen counter and spread her legs wide, fitting himself against her warm and wet opening. Betty's hands reached for his shoulders and clung there. Holding tight to each other, not kissing, their eyes melded together, he plunged deep.

Betty arched back releasing his shoulders and supporting herself on her elbows. Her hips lifted and fell in time with his rhythmic thrusts. Her head fell back as he watched her closely.

As he watched a pink flush spread up over Betty's chest, and she whimpered, Arnold's breathing quickened. His large hands spread over her chest trying to capture the widening blush. His thumbs met at her breastbone; his long fingers reached the place on either side of her where her breasts met her ribcage. As she tightened in climax, Arnold folded his arms around her back, enfolding her and held her tight while she bucked against his hips. His large hands moved down to encompass her buttock cheeks as he joined her in climax with two last powerful final thrusts.

Betty slumped against him, and he gathered her into his arms and carried her naked except for her white socks into the bedroom where he pulled back the covers, laid her down on the sheets and straightened to remove his own clothes. He crawled into bed with her and pulled her tight against him so no ounce of lonely space could intrude.

They didn't get to their meat loaf until midnight; and after eating, they slept until morning when Betty's alarm went off. Arnold dressed, kissed her lightly so as not to start anything, and left for his motel. There, he showered and went back to bed. When he opened his eyes, his first thought was to wonder if the restaurant was open.

CHAPTER 6

Arnold arrived at Linda Ivory's office at 11:00 AM. She greeted him with a hug. Hers was a toned-down beauty that Arnold appreciated. She wore her light brown hair long and pinned up, and her slender tall figure complemented the light blue skirt, white blouse and flat blue shoes she wore. She was also incredibly smart. Linda had been his investment advisor for a couple of years now and he was pretty sure he would always be in love with her. He loved her independence, her intelligence, and her ambition. But Linda had recently met a man through her work whom she loved, and she had married him.

Representatives from the accounting firm of David, Dixon and Connelly (D, D, & C) were scheduled to arrive at 11:30 AM to present their findings and a status report of their expectations for the up-coming quarter. Linda had prepared her accounting of deposit activity and revealed that the $2.5 million investment target had been exceeded due to higher than anticipated earnings in 6 of the 8 new investments. Her calculations indicated the total value of all the investments was $2.6 million, well on the way to the targeted goal of $5.0 million. She also pointed out that the number of wells that came online had exceeded the number quoted by the oil company.

"This amount is above and beyond the $1 million being transferred to the Alamosa Bank account for charity," Linda stated.

When the D, D, & C representatives arrived and made their presentation, there were no differences in account balances. The two representatives, Dan and Jacob, said they wanted to emphasize the need to open five other accounts that were beginning to show promise. After they discussed this with Linda and she agreed, she recommended the five to Arnold. Arnold gave her verbal approval to proceed.

Dan and Jacob assured him that D, D, & C was keeping the IRS up to date on quarterly tax submissions, so he had nothing to be concerned about from that direction. Then the two men complimented Linda on her efficient and timely handling of her work as they headed out the door. Linda grinned and asked Arnold if he was impressed with his earnings at the investment firm.

"I am delighted. It must not stop," he laughed.

Linda's demeanor became serious and she said, "We will be sure it does not through diversification. If there is one thing I have learned while working in investment programs, it is that you avoid putting too much of your money in one nest because it may disappear."

"So," she continued, "I would suggest you find a second and even a third investment firm other than ours in which to place your assets. You could easily accomplish this by asking Darrell to redirect a certain percentage of the revenue to the accounts you identify."

"I'll think on that Linda," Arnold promised, and he gave her a hug in parting.

It didn't take him long to see the wisdom in Linda's advice. He called D, D, & C from his hotel room, and they agreed and recommended five investment firms that would represent him well. He asked if D, D,

& C would continue to serve as his accountants and tax experts. They agreed that they would.

Arnold drove over to the bank and met with Darrell. He asked him to begin sending 5% of his revenue to each of the five different investment firms identified by D, D, & C effective immediately. Darrell agreed and said Arnold was wise to take such action.

"I'll be over to sign any of the necessary forms, tomorrow," Arnold promised.

As he was leaving the bank, Betty Walker entered.

"Hey Arnold," she called. "What are you doing this afternoon? I have the afternoon off and was wondering if you would enjoy seeing the calves being cared for by the 4H girls on Charlie Anderson's farm.

"Let's go," said Arnold.

They turned around together in the door and went to the parking lot where they took her car and left Arnold's rental. The farm was less than a half hour away from Calumet and when they got there, Arnold saw immediately that the calves were beautiful and were being taken care of properly.

"Charlie is providing the feed and water at no cost to the 4H group or to the girls or their parents," Betty commented as they looked over the small herd.

"That is very good," Arnold told her as they watched a worn out whitish grey car drive up.

"This is one of the 4H mothers now," Betty said. A tall slender young woman walked up to them carrying a bag of feed over her shoulder. Her long brown hair was straight and tied in a ponytail that hung down her back out of the hole in the back of her ball cap.

"Hi there Alex," Betty called.

"Hi Betty. I'm just dropping off some feed that had been recommended by the veterinarian."

She joined Betty and Arnold at the fence. Betty introduced her to Arnold as Alex Henry, the mother of Sally and Kathy. Alex let the feed bag slide down to sit on the ground at her feet.

"How are you making it with all the costs of school and 4H Ms. Henry?" Arnold asked.

"It is very difficult but very rewarding to experience taking care of the calf with my daughter Kathy," Alex replied. "I could use a higher paying job," she sighed. "It is nice to meet you Arnold. I'd best get this feed into the shed and head home." She picked the bag of feed up again and balancing it on her hip she opened a small feed shed and went inside.

"Alex is a 23-year-old single mother of two daughters. She has rent that is past due and over $200.00 in medical bills. Betty said quietly without being asked as the two of them continued to lean against the fence and watched Alex's old car drive away.

"How much is her rent?" Arnold asked.

"$100.00 a month," Betty responded.

Arnold spent another night with Betty and the next morning when she drove him back to his car in the bank parking lot, Arnold rolled what she had told him about Alex's finances over in his mind, thinking about how operating on such a small amount of money made a woman vulnerable to the slightest shifts of fate. If she fell, no one would be there catch her, and her daughters would go down with her.

When they arrived at the bank, Arnold went directly inside and requested that Darrell send Alex a check from the bank for $700.00. He also wanted someone from the bank to ask her each month if she needed assistance. If she did, he wanted the bank to provide what she needed out of his account without telling her who her benefactor was. He knew Darrell knew what to do, but he wanted to make sure, so he reminded him to keep his name confidential.

Saying goodbye to Betty, Arnold drove out to see Charlie Anderson to discuss the management of his eight sections of land.

Arnold drove out of Calumet into the countryside to look over the land that had once been his family's home. As he drove, he became anxious to tour the land he had walked over as a boy, back when he thought he owned the world.

Now, he did own part of it.

Arnold phoned Charlie to see if he wanted to meet him for a late lunch or dinner, giving Arnold time to walk across the original quarter of land where he was raised. Charlie told him to "have at it" and take as much time as he wanted.

"Just give me a call when you are ready to chat, and I'll meet you. I have a horse you could use to ride across the land," Charlie offered.

"Thanks for the offer Charlie. I think I'll walk like I did a long time ago."

"I understand," Charlie said and hung up.

Arnold turned in at the gravel drive that was the entrance to the farm. There was once a wooden sign there that said, "Barkley's Dairy and Farm." The sign had long ago faded and fallen over in a windstorm. It must have been hauled off because Arnold did not see even a pile of wood shavings where the sign used to stand.

The farm road was lined with fences on both sides and ended in a turnaround where two outbuildings stood on one side of the circle and the foundation that had once supported his family's home could be seen on the other. Arnold could see the results of Charlie's management in the many fences that had been down last time he was here that were now straight and tight. There was no house though. It had burned down and had never been replaced. The foundation was overgrown with tall grasses and weeds. A bed of irises his mother must have had planted had survived the fire and the passage of time. They were not blooming now, in September, but their spiky leaves, dried on the tips stuck out above the grasses that had been laid down by the wind.

Arnold got out of the car and wandered around the two barns. When he was here last, he had thought he was here to stay, and he had Black

Shadow with him. He had put Black Shadow in the fenced pasture, so the horse had access to the old barn for shelter. He had pitched a tent for himself in the lean-to off the barn.

The stalls were dusty, and cobwebs drifted from the ceiling rafters. Sunlight shown through the spaces, between the boards. When he was a kid, Arnold remembered riding his horse across the fields and along all the roads in the area. He had spent a lot of time on his sturdy cow pony, Smoky.

The farm was completely different from the Beth Ranch in Colorado. The grass was not so lush and there were no Ponderosa pine forests sighing in the wind. This piece of ground was home, though, a place where he, his siblings and parents had labored many hours, sweated through many hot and dusty hours loading hay and milking cows, worrying where their next meal was going to come from. Arnold opened a barbed wire gate and drove across the pasture to a pond that was partially overgrown with cattails and stopped on the dam and got out to walk. He had been here last August before Beth had her emergency surgery. That was when he had gotten called back to Colorado to help her.

As he walked over the farm, pictures of the past came to his mind. He didn't feel emotional about his memories now that he was here, standing on the land. Perhaps it was not the past he longed for, but the land, and now that he was here, he didn't long for what he had.

Alone with his thoughts, he sat and listened to the silence. There was nothing around him but red dirt and tall half dried grass rustling in the wind. It was comforting at first, but his mind wandered into thoughts about his divorce from Charlene and all the trouble caused by her ex-boyfriend and his attorney. He struggled to free himself from that quagmire, telling himself he had thought enough about that old crisis. He was through with the anger and the hate and had moved on to a better state of mind, one that involved helping others who sometimes cannot help themselves. Now, he could only thank his Savior, Jesus Christ, for the ability and resources to help others; and he was doing that.

Arnold walked around the old farmstead on his own for a couple of hours. Taking deep breathes of the country air, he meandered over the vanishing roads that crisscrossed the farm. He walked out in the pastures to stand on the banks of his two favorite fishing ponds where he smiled at the memories of huge bass and crappie tugging on his line and skinny dipping in the hot summers. He inspected the roof of the barn and the foundation of the house he had been raised in. His father's words, "always do what is right," echoed across the years.

Arnold walked until he was exhausted and hungry. He called Charlie to say he was ready to meet him for what would now be dinner because it was so late.

Charlie looked weary when Arnold arrived. His light denim work shirt and jeans were dusty and stained. Sweat made dark ovals under his arms. His curly brown hair was flattened in a circle where his hat had been sitting all day.

Never one to mince words or engage in small talk, Charlie spoke right up. "Arnold, I need a hand to handle coordination and oversight on the work I am hiring other outfits to perform. Do you know anyone who would be good at that job?"

"Would you be willing to train someone for the job?" Arnold asked, smiling and shaking the big man's hand. The two men were of similar size and age and each respected the different talents the other had.

"Yes. I would be willing to train someone. Then I would get what I want." Charlie said.

"You always get what you want around here, Sugar," the waitress said with a snort as she placed menus and water in front of the men.

"I do know that. Winnie Lea. The best steaks this side of Denver and the best whiskey this side of Tennessee." Charlie drawled, looking the woman up and down in a pretend come on.

"And who is this other handsome man?"

"Winnie Lea. This is Arnold Barkley, a lady's man and farmer from out near Calumet."

"Nice to meet you Arnold. What will you two have?"

"Likewise, Winnie Lea. I'll have a sirloin with potatoes and green beans and coffee black," said Arnold.

"I'll have the sirloin with potatoes and a tossed salad Winnie Lea. And bring me a shot of Jack Daniels with a cup of coffee," Charlie added.

As soon as Winnie Lea left with their order, Arnold said, "I recommend Alex Henry." "She is one of the 4H mothers. Do you know her? Do you think she can do the job?"

"I had not thought of a woman, but why not. I do know Alex. I'm sure she can do it," Charlie said.

"How much do you intend to pay?" Arnold asked.

"About $2.00 per hour. As little as possible really, and I can throw in an old pickup for her to drive."

"I'll help you afford Alex. But you have to keep my involvement a secret," Arnold offered. "I suggest you pay her $4.00 per hour and let her drive the pickup home and use it for her personal use as well as on the farm. What do you say?"

"I'll call her and discuss it with her immediately."

Arnold told him how pleased he was with the progress made on the farm and they discussed other projects Charlie saw that needed to be done around the old place. Arnold told him about working on plans for a house. Their dinners arrived and both men focused on food and coffee and whiskey for a while. Arnold left for the motel and a restful night of sleep.

The next day began with a bang when Betty called before his alarm went off and invited him to have breakfast with her and Alex in Calumet at 7:30 AM.

Arnold showered and shaved and drove to Calumet where he joined the two women at their table in Burly's Diner. As Arnold and Betty drank coffee, Alex began excitedly describing her new job with Charlie Anderson. She could hardly eat because she talked so much and so fast.

Arnold knew she would learn quickly and make Charlie a good employee.

CHAPTER 7

After the ladies left, Arnold remained at Burly's diner and drank another cup of coffee and sketched a rudimentary plan for his new house on the tablecloth that was made of butcher paper. He was going to avoid telling anyone about his decision to build a house until he could be sure of what he wanted. That way he could avoid others telling him what to do and how to do it.

Arnold returned to his motel, picking up blank drawing paper about 24 inches square from a department store on the way. He began sketching his ideas. The first four drawings taught him he was not an artist or a person who could draw out his thoughts very well. He did not give up. He dabbled and sketched and threw the sketches away only to begin again. Soon, he could see his ideas emerging and continued until he saw on the paper his dream house on the farm. He did not break for lunch or dinner. The final sketch was not pretty, but it was sufficient to show to a contractor who would know how to fix it. He saved one version, put it in the car so he would not forget it in the morning and went to bed.

He slept very restfully and awakened before the sun came up ready for a large breakfast. After breakfast, he drove to the farm and picked out the precise location where he wanted to build his home. He looked to the west, then to the south and east and north. The location he had chosen provided a clear view of the countryside in all directions. He dreamed of watching his own herd of black-angus cattle and a couple of horses graze out of the windows of his own home.

While he was sitting in his car daydreaming, he observed a pick-up approaching across the prairie. He thought it was Charlie Anderson, but it turned out to be Alex Henry in the truck Charlie had given her to use. She spotted Arnold and drove over to tell him about her new job. She was excited and leaned out the truck window to show him the two pages of notes she had taken so she would not forget all her job responsibilities.

"Charlie paid me an advance of $500.00," she chortled. "Can you believe it. I'll be able to buy food to keep us until the next pay day."

Arnold grinned up at her from his car window and congratulated her. She drove away in a plume of red Oklahoma dust.

He stayed where he was until noon and continued dreaming about his house plans. He wondered if he would have a wife to share this house with. He promised himself that he would call Brenda from the motel later. He made a couple of final corrections on the drawings and departed to track down a contractor.

Arnold called a contractor Charlie suggested and arranged to meet him at Burley's Diner in Calumet for afternoon coffee.

"I'm becoming a regular there," Arnold thought as he hung up the phone and locked his motel room behind him.

The contractor's name was Fred Rainy. He was a thin wiry man, freckled, with greying red hair that he covered with a grey ball cap and a think grey mustache hiding his top lip. He wore work boots, jeans, and a denim vest with pockets over the top of which stuck up straight edges and pencils. Fred sipped his coffee and reviewed the drawings Arnold had prepared. He made faces as he studied and wiggled thick bushy eyebrows, out of habit Arnold supposed.

"Before I start," Fred began, "I want to know if you have thick skin. I don't want to critique what you don't want me to critique."

"I made the drawings for you to critique. I expect it, and I have thick skin." Arnold took a sip of his own black coffee.

Fred and Arnold worked back and forth on the drawing until Fred said he thought they had a good idea of what Arnold wanted and he would take the drawing with him to have one of his employees, a draftsman, finalize it for Arnold's approval. Fred said the employee would drop the drawing off with Arnold at his hotel the next morning.

Fred and Arnold agreed to meet at the Burly Diner again the next morning to go over the final changes and layout the utilities and sewer.

The next morning, Fred's employee showed up right on time and reviewed the drawing with Arnold. Arnold tentatively agreed to five changes they had incorporated into the drawings. He then returned to the Burly Diner to meet Fred, drawing in hand. They discussed the changes he had agreed to and then discussed the availability of utilities and sewer.

Fred explained he would need to install lateral lines leading from a storage facility that would allow the sewage to leach into the ground. He told Arnold that the lateral field would need to be down gradient of the drinking well. Arnold pointed out on the drawing where the drinking water well was on the farm in relation to the house. They then determined where the electrical lines would come in.

"How do you plan to pay for supplies and labor?" Fred asked.

"How much do you expect the entire project to cost?" Arnold asked.

"Between $150 and $100,000.00."

"I'll pay 10% in advance and the balance when the county approves occupancy."

"When do you want to occupy the house?"

"In eight months."

The two men agreed, and Fred followed Arnold to his bank so Arnold could pay the first installment.

Arnold drove out to the farm again and dreamed of what his house would look like standing on the slight rise he had chosen. He could hardly believe he was going to have a home on the farm. He sat on the hood of his rental car and dreamed until it started to get dark.

His business in Oklahoma was completed. He had four days left before his flight back to Colorado. Should I call Betty, he wondered, or reschedule and head home? His father's admonition to him to always do the right thing, passed through his thoughts. His conscience began to plague him about the morality of his commitments to so many different women. Well, there are no formal commitments at least, he thought.

Unable to decide what to do, he headed toward his motel. He was fairly certain that Beth would not greet his decision to build a house in Oklahoma with gladness. She would not be happy. I should head to Colorado in the morning, Arnold decided, and on the way, I'll think of some way to sweeten this bit of news.

When he arrived at the motel, he called the airlines and rescheduled his return trip for the next morning. He then called Brenda in Denver.

She answered.

"Brenda, how are you doing? This is Arnold, remember me," he laughed.

"You idiot, of course I remember you. How are you doing?"

"I am in Oklahoma right now. I just designed a farmhouse that I hope to have done by next spring. It is on my old farm place."

"That is wonderful Arnold. I miss our farm. Dad would never have wanted to live in the city. I'm getting pretty tired of it myself. All noise and business. No animals or crops to care for."

"Are you thinking of leaving Denver?"

"Yes, but I have not decided yet where to go."

"Is the Chaplain still there?" Arnold could not help but ask.

There was a stiff silence on the phone for a moment before Brenda answered. "He is, but I think he will be transferring back to his old hospital soon." She changed the subject, "I've been working in the office at the hospital since we last talked. I've learned to keep books and bill patients."

"Are you going to leave with the Chaplain?" Arnold asked before he could stop himself. He knew Brenda was disappointed that he could not trust her or respect her privacy.

"Arnold. I have no intention of speaking about the Chaplain with you. That has not changed."

"I know, but I can't get it out of my head that you are sleeping with him, having sex to be specific. I would love to ….. Damn it Brenda, I'd love to start over, but if you are seeing the Chaplain, I can't share you."

"I know Arnold. No one is asking you to share."

"Brenda?"

"Goodbye Arnold."

Arnold looked at the phone then threw the hand piece back in its cradle. He hoped it didn't break or he would be paying for it. He muttered to himself as he packed his suitcase for the next morning. "Why couldn't you leave it alone? Why couldn't Brenda just tell me straight out what she and the Chaplain are doing? Why is she still in Denver? Why can't I trust her? She is not sexually experienced like Beth and Shoo Ann. But he knew she really liked sex."

He laid down and dropped into a sleep that was anything but peaceful.

CHAPTER 8

As the plane left the runway, Arnold fell sound asleep. The voice of the stewardess woke him when she announced that the plane was arriving in Pueblo.

Arnold found his truck in the parking lot and headed for Alameda, looking forward to seeing Beth and the ranch. Before he left the town of Pueblo, he stopped at a small restaurant and ate a hearty lunch with hot coffee to dispel the last of the grogginess caused by his early morning nap.

It took two hours to drive to the Beth ranch. As he drove, he marveled at the clear blue sky and the chiseled mountains that framed it on all sides. Beth did not know he was coming home early so he was hoping to surprise her.

Beth, surprised and happy, ran out to his truck to welcome him. She covered his face and lips with kisses. Arnold grinned from ear to ear. Beth was a fabulous kisser, probably the best kisser in the world.

How could he have forgotten that in less than two weeks? He wondered.

The ranch was beautiful, and after a brief rest, Arnold suggested they all go for a ride while the weather was so accommodating. As Shoo Ann,

Alice, Beth, and Arnold walked across the yard to the barn, Arnold called Black Shadow to him. The stallion came trotting up to the fence shaking his head and snorting. Autumn Time with Alice's pony, Sweetheart, and Shoo Ann's horse followed the big stallion up to the fence, then wheeled away and bucked and kicked playfully at each other.

"Shoo Ann. Have you named your pony yet?" Arnold asked.

"No. I have not." Shoo Ann answered stoutly.

"Well I guess Alice's horse is still called Sweetheart. Am I right?"

"Yes." Alice called out.

"You know, I named Black Shadow because I had a vision of the horse slipping like a shadow through the darkness," said Arnold.

"I know. You told us," Shoo Ann scolded. "I have not had a vision yet."

Arnold threw his arm over the stallion's neck and stroked his mane and forelock. The big stallion lowered his head and rubbed it gently against Arnold's chest. Arnold felt warmth spread through his veins. He knew horses were trained to behave in this way, to lower their heads in submission and to be gentle around humans, but somehow, he felt that there was more than training between Black Shadow and himself. There was real affection. He felt close to Black Shadow, almost as if the horse were a family member, maybe closer than that if truth be told. Arnold had no family left. No family by blood anyway. All his siblings had died early of disease or accident, and his parents had passed away too. Somewhere there was a cousin. He had a living cousin, but he didn't know where.

Arnold helped the ladies saddle up. Beth rode Autumn Time. He helped her lift her saddle and tighten the girth. She was still in the recovery stage of her surgery, and he didn't want her loosening any internal stitches. He gave Shoo Ann a hand although she really did not need it, and he gave Alice a couple of pointers after she had all her tack on the horse. Both Shoo Ann and Alice were careful learners and hard workers.

Arnold and the three ladies, rode to what had become everyone's favorite spot on the ranch, a spot among the trees where a spring flowed and warm fall grass and a few late flowers lined the bank of a little stream. As he dismounted and stretched, he noticed Alice hugging her pony. He smiled. She was building that bond that grew when horse and owner work closely together.

Alice wanted to train her pony, now called Sweetheart, to stay close to her whenever she dismounted. She dropped the reins in front of her on the grass. She talked to her pony, giving the mare verbal instructions to stay put, followed by a gentle push against her chest. He wondered how she was going to handle leaving the pony when she returned to her home in Chicago where she did not have a place to keep a horse.

He stopped himself on that thought. Let the moment be as it is and experience the joy of it, without worrying about when it all would end.

Beth and Alice groomed their horses and spread blankets on the grass. They laid down and beckoned Arnold to join them. He did not resist long. Their invitation was irresistible. When Black Shadow sniffed Alice's horse, Alice asked Arnold "Why does Black Shadow continue to sniff Sweetheart when they have already mated?"

"Well, she is a female and Black Shadow is a male. Black Shadow will pursue her until he is sure she is pregnant. Then he will not have any remaining responsibilities toward her. In the wild, the Stallion always acts as if he owns the mares in the herd especially for mating purposes."

"Do men think that way too," Alice asked.

Beth answered. "Yes. You better believe it. They want to own you whether or not you want to be owned."

Shoo Ann added, "Some-times that is not so bad."

Arnold stretched out on the blanket and stayed silent. He enjoyed the chatter. He knew he had a good deal, three beautiful women all to himself, and the idea of ownership never surfaced. He knew the ladies also enjoyed what they had.

The breeze was cool, but the warm sun kept everything warm. Arnold dozed comfortable feeling the warmth of Beth's body next to him on the blanket. She wanted to talk.

"How did your business go in Oklahoma?

"The business is doing well and is well organized with the bank directing the monthly deposits to 5 more investments to ensure the diversification of the money invested."

"Why is it important to put money in several accounts versus one large one," Beth asked.

"It is a good practice to guard against a total loss in case of corruption, misuse or misdirection of the account," he explained. "This way, I can lose one account without losing all my assets."

"Do you think it is important to change the ownership of the accounts to include me in addition to you? "

"Why would I do that? We are not married, and according to the law, I do not need to put your name on the account yet, but if they ever get married, I will add your name to the account to assure your part ownership. When we are married, we will enter into a legal arrangement called "joint tenancy.""

"I must remember this when we get married," Beth replied.

Arnold remained silent because he did not want to encourage that line of thinking even though he was starting to look more favorably on marriage than he had for a while.

Beth was a beautiful and wonderful woman and he knew it, but he still thought of Brenda from time to time. He laid closer to Beth, and they snuggled.

Arnold thought, this is the good life.

While Arnold and Beth reclined on the blanket and soaked up the autumn sun, Shoo Ann and Alice mounted their horses and started riding farther east.

"We will see you love birds in a while," Shoo Ann called to them. "We want to explore the ranch."

Within minutes of their disappearance, Beth began to undress Arnold and stroked his bare skin. Arnold encouraged her. He had not had sex with Beth in a long time. He could not contain himself for long once Beth extended her strokes to his penis. Her touch alternated between barely more than a tickle and a firm massage. Both were naked in a flash. Arnold entered her swiftly. Beth wrapped her legs around him and clung, not interested at all in slowing him down. She gasped as her body stretched to accommodate his large engorged member. Her newly made vagina needed more stretching and Arnold was happy to provide that.

Once the initial urgency passed, Arnold laid beside Beth on the blanket and stroked the purple scars that crisscrossed her groin. Her triangle of pubic hair was as thick as it had been when she had a penis, but now it cushioned the organs of a female. His thick finger explored. Some parts of her were numb, but others tickled, and she giggled. He moved his finger through her pubis like a comb and found the moist labia that were swollen from their previous love making. He stroked them and swirled his fingers around the nub of her clitoris. She watched him. Her arms crossed behind her head. Her eyes half closed.

"Does that arouse you? Do you have an orgasm now that you are a female?" Arnold asked quietly.

"Sometimes. Most of the time. The doctor told me that the sensitive part of the penis I used to have, its tip, is now at the bottom of my vagina, but it is still sensitive. They created the clitoris from the part of the penis that is erectile and can stiffen. These tissues are both sensitive to touch."

"Hmm. Let's give it another whirl."

Beth chuckled until her laugh was cut short by the sensations his delicate tracing on her clitoris caused. He slipped his little finger inside her to touch the nerves at the very deepest part of her. She yelped and rose to cling to him.

"Did that hurt?"

"No. Well, it felt so good that it felt like pain for a moment as if the tissue there is too sensitive. But now, I am hungry for more. Please don't stop."

Arnold lightened his touch until she pressed her body against his finger. He caressed her as long as he could with his fingers. When he could wait no more because of his own arousal, he moved over her and slipped inside her vagina, feeling its tightness hoping it never became blocked or closed to him.

Beth and Arnold lay entwined, legs around hips, arms around shoulders, worn out. They were about to drift off into sleep when they heard the warning hoot, "Whoo Hoo" that Shoo Ann gave.

They quickly stood, staggered a little, and Arnold yelled back, "Hold off a minute. Let us get ourselves together here."

They heard giggling from behind the trees as they dressed.

Dressed and mounted again, Beth gave the all clear to the two younger women and the four horses milled around together before heading back towards the ranch house and the barn.

As horses always are, they were eager to get back to their hay and oats, so the ride back was swift.

Shoo Ann and Alice slipped into their native language and chattered excitedly as the horses kept up a steady trot. Arnold could not understand what they were saying, but they sounded happy, totally comfortable in their world, and unconcerned with eavesdroppers like himself. He was happy to be a part of such joy.

At the barn, the riders brushed down their horses, gave them hay and oats, and made sure their water buckets were full of fresh cool water.

Arnold gave Beth a hand with the heavier work. Later, after the horses had eaten their fill and rested, Arnold would come back out and turn them into the larger pasture so they could roam.

While in the barn, he counted the number of bales of hay and decided it was time to order more because he did not want Jerry to run short feeding the new baby calves and new mothers. He mentioned this to Beth, and she agreed. Arnold called the Auction House from the house phone and ordered more hay.

They had just hung up when the phone rang. Arnold answered it. Without preamble, Charlie Anderson asked if he would object if he built a barn for the 4H girls to house their steers.

"I don't mind," Arnold informed him, "but keep a record of the costs for tax purposes."

On the other end of the line, Charlie agreed to keep the record.

"How are things going with you and Alex?" Arnold asked.

"Very good. She is performing well. Betty is talking about increasing the number of girls applying for 4H membership, so I'll need the help."

"I'll support whatever number Betty comes up with and you can handle," Arnold replied.

"Thanks Boss."

Arnold hung up.

Arnold went back outside and poked around in the outbuildings until he found Jerry.

"Hey Jerry. Will you be around for the delivery of more hay in a week?"

"Sure, I'll be here, and I'll make sure it is stacked in the barn," Jerry said amicably.

Later that day, when Beth and Arnold were sitting on the porch as the sun went down, Beth drinking herbal tea made by Maggie and Shoo Ann while Arnold drank scotch out of a short glass, Beth commented that she was beginning to become comfortable with Jerry working the ranch and helping reduce the amount of work for her to worry about.

"I think he is doing a great job," Arnold agreed.

"Would it bother you if I become close to him?"

"How close do you mean?" Arnold asked. "Are we talking about you sending cookies to his mother or are we talking close romantically?"

"Well I was thinking about sleeping with him. He is not married."

The hair on the back of Arnold's neck and arms stood up. "I would object seriously," he croaked. "I do not want the two of you involved sexually. How can you think I would not mind?"

"I was just wondering," Beth said.

"Were you involved with Jerry while I was gone to Oklahoma?"

"No."

He looked her over carefully. He believed her and decided not to dwell on it. He liked Jerry. He did not like the idea of this complication. He did not like the idea at all.

Arnold decided he had to pay more attention to Beth. He wasn't sure how much sex she wanted, but he wanted to make sure she was having as much as she wanted and that she was getting it from him. Over the next two days, Arnold approached Beth sexually several times a day.

Lying in bed, one afternoon, naked, while they were tangled in the sheets and tangled with each other, Beth asked Arnold if he was making love to her so much because she had raised the Jerry question.

"Yes," Arnold responded. "I don't ever want you to want sex without getting it."

Beth chuckled. "Don't worry you are definitely fulfilling my needs."

Arnold lay back on the pillow and thought. Why do I want sex so often? He wondered.

No matter, whenever the thought of sex crosses my mind, I'm approaching Beth. Maybe we will never get out of bed.

CHAPTER 9

B eth called David at the Alamosa bank for an update on what she and Arnold called the Catholic Nun building for girls. She learned they wanted to schedule a meeting with her for early the next morning to finalize the interior design of the building. The meeting time was set for 7:30 AM because another meeting was also scheduled for 9:00 AM.

Beth asked Arnold to attend both meetings with her. The construction contractor would be in attendance and the nuns wanted to discuss the number of people expected to be hired to staff teaching and administrative personnel positions.

"You are much better with numbers and contractors than I am. I'd appreciate your presence," Beth said with a smile.

Arnold agreed to go with her to Alamosa. They left early the next morning with good hot coffee in their thermos and a simple breakfast of eggs and toast in their stomachs that Shoo Ann had gotten up early to fix.

As they arrived at the Bank of Alamosa, Arnold reminded Beth that he was not going to accept a leadership role of any kind. He wanted to work in the background and to remain anonymous.

"You, however, can accept any position you desire."

The conference room was half full when they arrived. Sister Theresa, Sister Mary Joseph, and Sister Mary Frances were there already. The nuns hugged Beth and shook hands with Arnold as they came into the room. The sisters were dressed in their habits of brown and white and chattered excitedly about the plans for the school.

City and county officials were also there to give their approval of the site drawings and plans. Everyone present seemed to be overjoyed with the prospects of taking care of the young girls.

The construction representative reported that all permits had been approved, including road and street design. He announced that grading would start within a week. The city and county representatives agreed that all the permits were in place and announced plans for groundbreaking ceremonies. Everyone was encouraged to attend because the newspapers would have reporters at the ceremony.

Beth was as pleased as anyone with the state of the project. She, Arnold, David Baker and the sisters crossed the busy street to find some coffee at the nearest diner and continue talking there.

"I think I'd like to run for a position at the county that would oversee this project." Beth remarked after they had ordered coffee. "I don't know if that would be a conflict of interest though since I am providing the land. The city and county said they were going to need to fill three positions soon. I'm interested in one of them."

Arnold and the sisters encouraged her to pursue whatever position she desired.

"You are an outstanding advocate for the people of the County and for the girls attending the school. You belong to the county, and you have the imagination to think about what the girls' lives must be like," Sister Mary Joseph, commented.

"What if I don't have what it takes?" Beth asked, becoming nervous at the idea of a position in charge of something.

"You'll do great. However, you can always resign," Arnold reminded her.

Everyone drank silently for a while, enjoying the strong black coffee as they entertained their own thoughts.

"I'll bet you a silver dollar that many comments and changes are in store for the main teaching area due to its size," Arnold predicted.

"We will see," replied Beth.

"Have you seen the local newspaper," asked Sister Theresa?

"Why, what's going on?" asked Beth.

"The Catholic Church is planning to close St. Pius, their school and church north of the City. Our hearts are breaking."

Arnold raised his head from his coffee cup when he heard that. "The population of the new facility will probably not remain twenty or less for long once the children from the closed Catholic school start attending the new facility south of the City. Looks like the teaching area might be too small," he said with a wink at Beth.

"Did you already know that when you bet there would be changes. You rogue!" laughed Beth.

After a brief three days, the banker called a special meeting of the Catholic nuns, city and county officials, construction contractor and anyone else who was interested in attending to discuss the closing of the current Catholic School north of town and the possible effect this would have on plans for the new facility south of the City.

Beth and Arnold attended. When the meeting began and was officially opened for new business, the nun who spoke as a representative of the teachers at the old school spoke and cautioned everyone about approving plans that failed to meet the needs of the teachers at the start because it would always restrict the number of girls that could be accommodated at one time.

The city and county representatives both insisted that the current level of attendance remain 20 or less. "If we must, we will prohibit any transfer of students from the school that is closing to the new building to protect the project."

A low grumbling filled the room.

The representative from the Catholic Church shouted, "We want to withdraw our support for the new building if it will not take in the students from St. Pius."

"Your original $5 million is already allocated, and it is non-refundable," David Baker stated.

"I've decided not to pursue the city or county positions that are open," Beth whispered to Arnold. "I do not want to be involved with the controversy brewing. It will surely adversely affect the quality of the project."

"Relax and allow some time for the emotions to settle before you make a final decision," Arnold advised.

For now, they agreed stay calm and wait for more to unfold before they became involved further. Both Arnold and Beth were becoming skeptical of the other individuals who were involved and began thinking about withdrawing their support.

On their way home, Arnold informed Beth he was planning a camping trip and wanted to know if Beth was interested in going along.

"I am happy to be home. Your camping trips contain great scenery and good camping but each time it becomes tiring and you become discontented."

"I do travel farther than I intend to or should," Arnold admitted. "What if I take shorter trips from now on would you come with me?"

"I don't know. I like to stay home," Beth insisted.

Arnold eyed her out of the corner of his eye as he drove. This relationship issue continued to bother him. Once he had allowed someone to slip up on him, Charlene, and he swore it would never happen again.

I keep thinking it might already be happening again, Arnold thought. Is it happening again? I want to believe Beth. But I wanted to believe Charlene once too. Look where that got me…divorced and in court to save my assets. The situation with Beth is clearly different because I promised I would help her. I am determined to do the right thing. That is the code I adopted to live by.

As Arnold fretted over whether he could trust Beth, he concluded that he would continue to help her, but he might not continue to love her.

I was deceived once, he thought. It will never happen again; at least not to me.

Arnold began to think of ways to protect himself, to keep his eyes and ears open for signs; to be observant of Jerry and Beth and assess their behavior, while trying to control and keep his sanity. He thought of talking to Beth about it, and he became depressed.

If it is happening again. I cannot stand still and let it happen. I will talk to Beth as soon as we get back to the ranch.

An hour after they got home, Beth was sitting on the couch listening to the radio. He approached her.

"Can we talk for a while?" he asked.

Arnold began slowly and purposely. "I am really troubled by the question you asked concerning Jerry and you establishing a romantic relationship," he began.

Beth took in a deep breath and began to cry. "I am so sorry that I even asked the question. Please forget I ever asked."

Her crying intensified and became deep chested sobs like convulsions.

"Please forget I asked. Please forgive me," she repeated. "Please forget I asked. Please forgive me."

Arnold wrapped his arms tightly around her, trying to settle her down. The violence of her emotions frightened him.

"Calm down please. Hold on to me. Everything will be all right," he whispered. "I love you. I can't stand to see you so upset."

Beth tried to get her sobs under control and look Arnold in the eye, but each time she met his gaze, she lost it again and wept bitterly. Arnold kept holding her tight. It took a long time, but she finally started to breathe somewhat normally. Beth went to the bathroom then returned.

Arnold took her back into his arms and her eyes filled with tears again.

"Is there anything I can do or say that would convince you that I am sincere and truly sorry?" she asked.

"I'm sorry, because I like Jerry and he is a good worker, but I think you must fire Jerry Walker when he arrives to work in the morning. No tears. No apologies. No 'I am sorry Jerry.' Just say 'Jerry you are terminated as of this moment.' Then you must walk away, solid in your conviction that you did the right thing."

Beth looked him in the eye and said, "Arnold, I will do that in the morning."

Arnold got up from the couch, went in the kitchen and poured them both a strong, black, hot cup of coffee. They sat side by side and silently drank every drop.

Arnold silently prayed that his Lord and Savior had intervened in the situation and had taken control of and was directing their lives. Beth was truly deserving of his forgiveness. He vowed to go forward with faith, less anxiety, and more trust in the future. He assured himself he was doing the right thing.

"Beth. I believe you. This issue is truly behind us and will never surface again."

Beth's breathing slowed to a gentle rhythm. They hugged each other and fell asleep together on the couch

Arnold woke up around 3:30 AM, made coffee, dressed, and sat in front of the typewriter, but did not type anything. He decided to go into town and get a paper to read as soon as it was light. Then, he would go to the bank. He wanted to avoid thinking about the events of the day before. He did not want to be present when Jerry arrived for work. He wanted Beth to have total privacy when she fired him.

Arnold went out to his truck and headed over to Maggie's restaurant for a good breakfast, drove around the country roads for a while, then headed to town. They were a few days into the month of October now and the weather had turned chilly, but they had not had any snow yet. Upon his return to the ranch, he saddled Black Shadow and went for a cold and breezy ride. The temperature was really too cool for a comfortable ride, but he needed privacy for himself as much as Beth did for herself. He rode to his favorite spot on the ranch and built a nice warm fire beside the little stream and began to feel better. He was out of the wind in this low spot between the trees. He threw on another log for good measure. He put two thick blankets on the extra wood he had collected and made himself a back rest against which he could lean and face the fire.

Watching the flames lick at the wood, he reviewed the conversation from the night before and let thoughts from the last evening cross his mind at random. He wanted to think of a way to avoid confronting Beth with any of this ever again. Arnold thought Jerry's absence from the ranch would make it easier for Beth to stay true to him. Eventually, out of sight out of mind would prevail and she would stop thinking about Jerry. He hoped.

He put another log on the fire. He was not ready to depart yet. He needed time to enjoy the quiet and peace while Black Shadow tore off mouthfuls of grass nearby. After a while, he noticed that he had built a very large fire.

How will I put his out before I leave? he thought. There was water in the small creek but getting some of it to the fire was going to be a cold challenge. He decided to let it burn down. He had gotten up too early and needed a short nap.

When Arnold woke up, Black Shadow was standing over him. Reins stroked his face. Arnold decided he liked his new alarm clock. The fire had burned down. Only a few coals remained. He got up and stretched, put the blankets back in the saddle bag, then mounted Black Shadow and rode to the barn. There, he gave the stallion a good rub down.

When he entered the kitchen, he found that Beth had prepared lunch for both of them. She gave him a hug and a smile.

Afraid to ask, he hoped that Jerry departed quietly, without making a scene.

CHAPTER 10

Charlie Anderson called Arnold the next evening as he sat at the dinner table enjoying a whiskey after supper.

"Boss, the owners of the two sections of land between the sections you own have approached me about selling their farms to you. They don't want Robert involved because they don't want to pay commission. I kind of understand that."

"I definitely want that land Charlie. We can handle the deal ourselves," responded Arnold. He sat up straighter in his chair as Charlie continued.

"I know the current owners well. They would like to continue living in their houses after they sell them. One family consists of two older adults who do not work out of doors much anymore. The other property owner is a woman in her 70's. She is very energetic. She raises a garden, takes care of 10 to 12 chickens for eggs, and milks a cow daily for her personal use. I don't want to buy the properties myself, but I'll take care of them for you with your other holdings."

"Thanks Charlie. I'll leave here as soon as I can get a flight. I'll handle the purchase of the two sections myself," Arnold said before hanging up.

Arnold took another sip of whiskey and looked across the table at Beth, where she was playing solitaire and sipping a cup of coffee. Outside, snow had begun to fall. You never could tell about the weather in the mountains in late October. One day it could be warm and the next icy.

"Beth, I'm going to Oklahoma to buy some more property as soon as I can get a flight. I want to check on the progress of the house I'm building there too. Would you like to come along with me? It will be a quick trip."

"Please excuse me from the trip Arnold," Beth answered. "The nuns may try again to work something out regarding the planned Educational Facility. I'd like to help if I can."

Arnold called the airline and got a seat on a flight going out of Pueblo the next day. He called Charlie and told him his arrival time. Charlie was pleased and said he would inform Robert to avoid any controversy.

Early the next morning, as Arnold walked to the barn, snow hit him in the face. He questioned his wisdom of traveling at this time of year. Once he was out on the road, he saw they were not in bad shape, but he had to go slow along several parts of the mountainous route. Arriving in Pueblo was a relief.

The flight crews were busy de-icing the wings when he took his seat on the plane. He wondered how the weather was in Oklahoma. Once they took off and reached cruising altitude, the flight was smooth, and Arnold went to sleep.

He woke up as the plane made its final descent. Looking out he realized that Oklahoma was also experiencing inclement weather. He picked up his rental car at the counter and drove slowly out of Oklahoma City to El Reno where he had reserved a motel room. He checked in but did not stay long. He drove on to Calumet to meet with Robert.

Upon entering Robert's office, Charlene informed him that Robert was in Nashville, Tennessee for a four-day conference and would return on Sunday. He called Charlie from Charlene's desk phone and they decided to meet with Charlie's people that afternoon.

"I've got two hours," Arnold told his ex-wife.

"Perfect!" Charlene smiled broadly and took his hand, leading him to the back office where she had installed a couch for napping. She loosened his tie and placed his large hand on her breast.

"I'll be right back. I've got to lock the front door and take the telephone off the hook," she whispered.

Charlene slipped back into the back office and began stripping out of her work clothes, hanging them carefully on the two hooks on the back of the door. Arnold watched as she pulled her stockings off and unzipped her black skirt. Her nylon panties were practically transparent. Her blouse was long shielding her to her hips.

Arnold took off his coat and tie as he kept his eyes on Charlene, not wanting to miss an inch as it was revealed. She was unbuttoning her blouse as he removed his belt and kicked off his shoes. She grinned at him.

His hands already remembered the feel of her smooth skin.

Charlene reached behind her and took off her bra, letting it drop away from her large breasts. Now she stood before him in only her panties.

He reached for her them and pulled her into his arms. They kissed as she unbuttoned his shirt and pulled it down over his big shoulders. Releasing the kiss, she pulled his winter t-shirt up over his head and ran her hands over his chest.

"Arnold. I have missed you," she sighed.

Arnold wasted no time in removing her panties and thought his penis would break through his pants zipper before she actually had it undone. In a tangle of hands, the two finally ended up naked.

Arnold sat down on the couch with Charlene's legs spread across his thighs. She was parted and open to him. He explored the velvet folds of her sex with his fingers. She arched in pleasure, holding onto him for support. He pulled her forward onto his lap and down on his engorged penis. She moved up and down and he pressed his lips against her neck, his hands on her buttock, pressing himself as deeply within her as he could get.

They came that first time quickly. Then, they stretched out on the cushions of the couch and explored each other piece by piece, leaving out nothing, breasts, nipples, bellies, hip bones, and collar bones. Charlene explored Arnold's penis until it was hard again.

"I always marvel at such length Arnold. Men are miraculously made."

Arnold had given up resisting Charlene. He had long ago forgiven her for her part in their divorce realizing that she had been hoodwinked by her lover and his lawyers. She was married to Robert now, but she still felt that Arnold's body belonged to her, and his body did not make a liar out of her. Physically, they knew each other so well.

Two hours later, dressed once again, Arnold met Charlie and his clients at a coffee shop in downtown Calumet. The meeting was cordial and friendly. Charlie introduced the man and woman as Mr. and Mrs. Kennedy and the woman alone as the widow Mrs. Wilson. All three were grey headed, thin, and weathered. Charlie briefly described previous conversations they each had had with him.

Mr. Kennedy informed Charlie and Arnold that he and his wife wanted to sell their section of land for $40,000.00 and the sales contract would contain language that would permit them to continue living in the house and otherwise occupying two outbuildings, one a work shop and the other a garage.

"I can agree to that provision," Arnold said, "as long as there is an end to your occupancy of the home and outbuildings. Perhaps the age of 95 for either of you is reasonable or upon the death of both, whichever occurs first."

They readily agreed and they shook hands.

I'll discuss this with the title company and have a contract drawn up," Charlie offered. Once everyone has reviewed and approved the contract, each of you will be asked to sign it along with Arnold as the buyer."

"Can we make the date for possession 5 days from now? Mr. Kennedy asked.

"Certainly," Charlie agreed at a nod from Arnold. They all were happy with that.

They turned to Mrs. Wilson.

"This makes things easy," she said ever so distinctly. "I'll have the same, with one exception. I want to retain 10 acres in addition to the house for my personal use. I raise chickens and I have a cow that I milk. I may also want a saddle pony to ride. Sometimes I dream I am 25 years of age instead of 70, if you know what I mean."

Charlie laughed and asked her if the price of $40,000.00 was ok for the section of land and if she was ok with the provision that she retains use of the house and 10 acres and outbuildings until she reaches 95 years of age or dies, whichever occurs first.

"I agree, said Mrs. Wilson.

"Will it be okay if the date of possession is five days from now for you as well? Charlie asked.

"I agree to that too," said Mrs. Wilson.

Mrs. Wilson and the Kennedy's departed and Arnold looked at his watch, noting the time. I'll meet you Charlie at Darrell's bank in an hour. That will make it simple to write a check for each property.

While writing the two checks at the bank, one to each seller, Arnold asked Darrell if the purchase was covered by the distribution from the investments.

"I calculated it last evening and believe you are okay," Darrell said, "but we are monitoring the activity and if we need to supplement, we will cover it."

Charlie arrived at the bank and confirmed the transactions connected each of the sections he owned into one tract of land. "Have you given any thought to what changes you want to make to the properties? He asked.

"I had better drive over the land and inspect it before making a decision, Arnold responded.

"I can send over Alex and her pick-up because it is a four-wheel drive," Charlie offered.

"That would be nice," Arnold agreed.

"When do you plan to drive over the new purchase? Charlie asked.

"When can I borrow Alex and the pick-up?"

"I'll get right back to you. I'll give her a call right now," Charlie responded.

After listening to Charlie discuss Alex's projects and priorities, Arnold suggested over his shoulder that breakfast at the restaurant in Calumet at 7:30 in the morning would be a good time to start, and they could be done by 4:00 PM.

Charlie relayed the idea to Alex, and she agreed.

"When we are done inspecting," Arnold said, "You and I will get back together to discuss my plans."

Arnold asked Charlie if he wanted to convert the new sections to grass and apply the same program being offered by the ASCS office to them.

"I think that will be a good idea. The rent for each of the two new sections would be the same as the other four sections. Have you given any thought to connecting all the land without the roads between each of the sections?"

"I don't think the County would approve it," Arnold said.

I think they might because they would not then need to maintain any of the roads thereby reducing their costs. The configuration is 2 miles wide and 3 miles long. I'll approach the County with the possibility, Charlie said

"Avoid committing to maintenance of the roadway as that would be costly," warned Arnold. "They should approve fencing across each roadway and closing each if they approve the concept."

Charlie nodded.

"Thanks for bringing these people to me Charlie and thanks for all your work. I've had a busy day and want to get back to the motel for some rest. I'll talk to you after Alex and I have toured the new properties."

As Arnold arrived at the motel, Beth called and wanted to know what was going on. Arnold informed her he had purchased two more sections of land and that the purchase connected his other purchases.

"I think, my ranch is still larger at 4,000 acres," Beth teased.

"I'll get even with you when I get back," Arnold threatened.

"Bring it on," she laughed, and they said good night and hung up.

Edward K. Mackendrik

CHAPTER 11

Arnold met Alex Henry at the Bull Horn Café in Calumet. The bell on the door rang as she stepped into the diner. To Arnold, her face looked brown and healthy above the corduroy collar of her canvas work coat. He knew she was 23 years old. She was slender. She had caught her straight brown hair up in a ponytail that hung down her back under a creased straw hat. A pair of gloves drooped out of her back pocket.

"Good morning Alex," Arnold greeted her as she crossed to the table he had occupied. "Thanks for agreeing to drive me around this morning. How are your daughters? How is your job going with Charlie?"

"Hello Mr. Barkley." Alex shook his hand and smiled. "I love my job and the girls are doing just fine."

"It's Arnold, Alex. Call me Arnold."

Over a quick breakfast of biscuits, gravy, and coffee, Alex told Arnold about the cows and the properties she took care of for Charlie, and she wondered out loud if Charlie would increase her wages with the additional sections to take care of. Arnold said he did not know.

Out in the parking lot, they got into the old grey work truck that Charlie had given to Alex to use on the job. It was dented and had rust streaks on it, but it was 4-wheel drive, its heater worked, and it was reliable. Alex shifted into first gear and they set out for the string of properties Arnold had purchased.

It was still Fall but felt like Winter. The cool weather had turned the grasses along the roads a dull tan and the trees were bare of leaves. A skiff of snow dusted the blacktop road and the prairie around it. He was quickly deciding to follow Charlie advice and convert the ground to grass for hay and pasture and raise cattle. He knew Charlie would be pleased.

After they turned down one of the dirt roads between the sections, Arnold noticed a dilapidated house under a grove of trees that he did not know was located on the property.

They approached the house and discovered people were living in it. Arnold knocked on the door. Alex stayed in the truck.

A woman answered the door and he could see in the room behind her other faces.

"Hi. I'm Arnold Barkley and I own this land. Who are you?"

One of the faces in the back came forward and became a young Hispanic woman in her late teens or early twenties.

"Sir. Only I speak Ing-les."

Arnold crossed the threshold and looked around the dim room. It appeared that five women and one man lived in the house, at least that is what he could see from the doorway. The house was small, so he did not think there were too many more people in the other rooms. All of them looked dirty, thirsty, and were probably hungry.

"Why are you here?" he asked.

"We have been living here for only a few days. No one knows we are here. We are not paying rent because there is no water or electrical power. Our car ran out of gas and we have no more food. If we can get some gas, we plan to leave in two days."

"Well Alex and I can give you a lift to El Reno for a can of gas and some food. Then you can leave. Would you, be willing to come with us?" Arnold indicated with a nod of his head that he was speaking to the young woman who spoke English not the whole room.

The side trip for gas took an hour. Alex drove and the young woman sat between her and Arnold. She said her name was Louise. When the trio got back to the abandon farmstead, they put gas in the car, and it started right up.

There were smiles all around. Alex went back to the truck. Louise asked Arnold into the house.

They had purchased hamburgers and fries for everyone in El Reno and everyone sat around the walls on the floor to eat the first meal they had had in a day or two. Arnold saw that they ate as though they were starved. Louise asked Arnold to go with her into one of the bedrooms. She firmly shut the door behind them and said she wanted to thank him and offered sex.

"No," Arnold assured her. "You do not need to pay me with sex." He gave her a $10.00 dollar bill and she kissed his cheek.

"Be safe," he said as he left the group at the front door. They all watched him get into the old truck with Alex. Arnold felt some satisfaction that he had done the right thing here as his father always admonished him to do.

It took another hour for Alex, and he to complete their assessment of the new sections.

As Alex drove into the parking lot of the diner to return Arnold to his rental car, Arnold asked her how her finances were doing.

"You asked earlier about a raise. Are you making enough money to get along?" he asked.

"Well if my ex-husband would pay his child support, that would help," she remarked.

"How much does he owe?" Arnold asked.

"Well he is supposed to pay $50.00 per month, but he has not paid anything the last year."

"Are you receiving money from the bank?" Arnold asked.

"Like clockwork," Alex admitted, "$600.00 every other month. This helps a lot, but it did not keep up with her expenses especially with the two girls."

Arnold looked her in the eye and asked, "Can you keep a secret?"

"Of course, I can," she replied.

"I'm going to give you some money that you do not ever have to pay back on the condition that you never tell anyone about it."

From across the cab, Alex stared at him in silence.

"Do we agree?" he persisted.

Tears spilled over the edges of her eyes as she nodded. Arnold opened his wallet and laid $600.00 in her hand. Her tears ran down her cheeks as she looked at the money in her palm.

"Alex. There is more where that came from. Be cool and work hard at your job with Charlie." He wrote a number on a scrap of paper she had on the dash. "Here is my phone number. Let me know if you need anything. I am returning to Colorado soon."

In his rental car, before he left the parking lot of the diner, Arnold called Darrell and asked him to increase Alex's allotment to $800.00 every month instead of $600.00 every other month.

That afternoon, Arnold quickly ran through the rest of his errands. He talked to Darrel and Linda and confirmed his investment portfolio. He contacted the builder, and they went over the drawings for his house. They reviewed the foundation and garage flooring layout at the site. He could not review the poured flooring because the weather was too cold for pouring concrete, so he excused himself and headed for the airport.

Arnold got on the airplane and located his seat realizing he had lucked out. The seat was only three rows from the front and adjacent to the window. He said to himself, "perfect."

He relaxed, ordered a Jack Daniel's with ginger ale, and immediately began to think over the events of the last week. His mind touched on Beth and Jerry. His mind bumped off that subject quickly. Then he thought of the construction of his new home in Oklahoma and lingered over that with anticipation and pleasure.

He ordered a second Jack Daniel's before they began to taxi.

The hostess delivered his drink almost immediately. When she handed it to him, he asked, "Are you planning to occupy this seat next to me?"

She winked and replied. "It would be my pleasure, but I better stay with my duties."

Only slightly disappointed for he knew his chances had been slim from the beginning, Arnold smiled and returned to contemplating the rich color of the whiskey in the small cocktail glass, and his thoughts returned to Beth.

He realized he might never understand Beth, but he knew he would keep trying because she was beautiful and bright and kind. Her figure alone, with breasts that would impress any clothes designer, kept him enthralled.

I should not complicate our relationship. Just relax and enjoy whatever occurs with her and be patient. It would also be helpful if you could think of her character without blaming her for the Jerry situation, he chided himself. She has been good to you from the beginning.

He noticed the plane was departing the airport and watched as the white lines on the runway sped by then receded to mere dots beneath his window. He glanced back into the cabin and realized he had lucked out. No one had sat down beside him. He noticed a new drink on the pulldown tray in front of the aisle seat and took a sip. The hostess must have set it there when he was watching take off. It was pure water. Later he asked the hostess about his drink.

"Why, I was hoping you would sleep in preparation for our arrival in Pueblo."

"Hmm. You're telling me that I might need to rest up then." He smiled, recognizing the message she was sending.

He slept well for the duration of the flight. When they deplaned at Pueblo, he purposely delayed getting up and lingered at the door. He fell into step beside the hostess as they walked down the jet-way and commented, "We meet again."

She laughed and handed him her small carry-on bag.

"I'll meet you at the baggage claim, she said."

He walked to the baggage claim, retrieved his luggage, and waited for the hostess. He didn't have too long to wait. Before long, he saw her heading towards him, her long legs shortening the distance between them in a hurry even though she did not seem to hurry. Her blonde hair was freshly fluffed around her pretty face.

As she reached him, she linked her arm in his and looked up at him. "Where too? My name is Mary Jo. I have a room at the Hilton."

Arnold took her arm and matched his gait to hers as they left the airport. He found his truck in the parking lot and settled her into the passenger seat. He stopped at a liquor store on the way to the nearby hotel and picked up some wine.

In her room, Mary Jo got out a wine opener out of her purse and Arnold twisted the cork out of the bottle. They sat down on the sofa and clinked their glasses together.

"What are we toasting?" Mary Jo asked.

"We are toasting strangers. Beautiful strangers," Arnold said.

"And, tall and broad strangers, I say," Mary Jo added. "There is no way I could pass you up cowboy."

Arnold laughed and reached for her glass. He set it carefully on the end table. Then he stood and reached down for her, lifting her bodily off the sofa. Her heels fell off her feet on the way to the bed. She reached her arms around his neck and just studied him.

He stood her beside the bed, pulled down the spread and the sheet, and ran his hands down over her hips. His fingers had caught the hem of her skirt so on their way up, his hands brought her skirt with it, exposing her long white legs to the cool air. He pinned the skirt under his forearms and went back down for her panties. This time his hands drug them and her hosiery downward. As the fabric passed her knees, she deftly stepped out of half of her clothes.

Arnold unbuttoned the back of her skirt and let it fall. He pushed up her blouse without unbuttoning it until it came off over her head. He dropped it on the bed and undid her bra, a skimpy thing that gave way easily beneath his fingers.

Arnold slowly moved his splayed fingers all over the curves of her body. She was smooth and soft. His fingers were rough. Once he discovered that MaryJo had undone the buttons of his shirt, he shrugged out of it. She splayed her fingers in imitation of his across the hard muscles of his chest and stomach, exploring, lingering at his belt to work at the buckle.

Reluctant to remove his hands from her luscious skin, Arnold took over undoing the buckle afraid it would take her longer to undo it than he had control. They were both very aware of the hard ridge pressing against the zipper of his jeans.

He pushed his jeans down and his penis sprung out, ready to go. He lifted Mary Jo up, spreading her legs around his waist and lowering her to the bed. He stretched out over her, pressing the weight of his body down on her. She wrapped her legs around his hips as his fingers investigated the warm wet cleft between her thighs.

She groaned and he answered by raising up and penetrating her swiftly. She was slick and ready. They moved together in a frantic first rhythm before slowing and breathing together nose to nose. He buried his face in her neck as she arched against him with all her strength, her climax leaving her taut as a bow, feeling without thoughts. He followed her immediately into the void, his stokes long and strong until he too arched and then fell to her side, his arms laying across her breasts.

They slept satisfied by their encounter. Hours later, as the sun came over the horizon, Arnold dressed and slipped out of Mary Jo's room. He found his truck and headed for The Beth Ranch.

CHAPTER 12

When Arnold arrived at the Beth ranch, he was feeling tired and irritated.

Maybe he was having too much sex, he thought.

He climbed out of his truck and the first thing he saw was Black Shadow standing near the pasture fence. His weary sadness left him as he approached the big horse. Black Shadow nudged him with his nose, welcoming him home. Somehow the stallion spoke his language. Arnold met Black Shadow's soft muzzle with his own cold nose, and beast and man exchanged their warm breath. It steamed in the chilly air. Arnold ran his hands over the horse's face and neck, digging his fingers into the stallion's thickening winter coat before turning and walking to the house carrying his luggage.

The living room was warm from the fireplace and cook stove in the kitchen. As he entered, Beth rushed to him and hugged him tight, pressing little kisses on his lips and cheeks. He lifted her up in the air and pressed his own cold lips into her warm neck. She squirmed in his grip. He nibbled at her ear lobe and made her laugh.

"You smell like perfume and sex," Beth said, stepping back from him.

"Nothing you need to worry about," Arnold replied as Beth studied him from head to toe, holding his hands in hers.

"Hmmm," Beth murmured. "You need a bath."

"After coffee," Arnold said calmly still smiling.

The two headed into the kitchen hand in hand, Beth for a refill of coffee and Arnold for his first cup of the day.

Arnold told her about the completion of the land purchase. She told him he had several pieces of mail waiting that probably needed a response from him. "Business can wait," he replied. "I'm just enjoying this coffee and your company. We have all the time in the world."

"Really?" she asked. "That sounds heavenly. If you are not too tired of traveling, I would like to suggest we go somewhere for a week, just the two of us. We need each other without interruption."

Arnold raised his eyebrow, "This is rare. You want to take a trip?"

Beth smirked. "It does seem odd. I am just tired of ranch responsibilities, and I have missed you. I also sense you need more sex." She pointed to her wrinkled nose.

"I will bathe, toss a clean set of clothes in my suitcase and grab my roadmap while you get dressed and pack. We will be on our way then decide where we are going."

Within 45 minutes the two were in his truck heading south, suitcases stashed in the bed of the truck. They decided to pick their destination over dinner. As soon as they hit Interstate Highway 25, they were headed south.

They stopped at a small café in Walsenburg Colorado, ate a light dinner, and decided to drive to Santa Fe, New Mexico. Arnold knew Santa Fe had several attractions from which they could choose. The driving distance was greater than they had expected but they really did not care. They were mainly concerned with finding a nice motel room with amenities to please both of them.

In Santa Fe, they found a hotel on the central town plaza. The attendant provided a comfortable suite for them. The bed was big and the headboard high, solid and painted with Indian designs. They had their own bathroom and agreed to stay a week. The attendant assured them they would be satisfied with the accommodations. Tired from the long day, they stretched out on the bed and slept first. They planned to play later.

Arnold awoke in the dark to soft nibbles on his chest and gentle tugs on his nipples. The sensations nearly sent him to the verge of losing himself. Beth calmed him. She stroked him. Her hands and lips on his body in the dark brought him back to the verge of climax. She climbed on top of him, positioned herself over his hips and slid down over his penis. Her newly crafted vagina was tight and warm. Arnold gasped for air. Beth let her smaller body ride the waves of his passion as he gave up control to her, his mind and body exploding.

Several minutes later out of the dark he croaked, "When did you learn that?"

"Years ago, from magazines and romance books," she giggled. "I guess they work pretty well. I'm only a beginner though. I'm going to spend the whole week practicing on you. I want to be perfect at making fantastic love to you."

After three days, she had convinced him that she had totally mastered the art of being a woman. Only the scars that punctuated her groin area gave evidence to her former dual sex. They extended their stay at the resort for one additional week and seriously considered another before Beth received an urgent phone call from the banker regarding the new facility being built with the nuns for homeless girls. They decided to depart in two days. Both were happy with their vacation.

As they pulled out onto the highway heading North for Colorado and home, Arnold asked, "By the way, who is watching The Beth Ranch while we are gone?"

He was slightly chagrinned that he had just now remembered that he had told Beth to fire Jerry the ranch hand. He had not even thought about their responsibilities at the ranch.

"Shoo Ann and Alice of course," Beth said.

"I want to alert you to the fact that I have placed an ad on the bulletin board at the restaurant for an experienced ranch hand to assist me in doing work at the ranch. She continued. "I identified three prerequisites or requirements for the person who takes the job. First, I want them to have a minimum of five years ranch work experience with cattle and horses; then, I want the person to be married and living close enough to commute daily to the ranch; and also, I want them to accept a reasonable salary with pay on each Friday."

She looked over at Arnold. "I hope this is acceptable to you. I plan to do interviews, and I'd like you to participate if you will."

"That all sounds like a good plan to me. I am willing to help."

"That is good because while we were in Santa Fe, I received a message from Shoo Ann saying someone had responded to my ad at the restaurant. We have an interview scheduled as soon as we get back because we will need help right away with winter coming on."

As soon as they arrived at the ranch, Arnold was welcomed by Black Shadow who appeared eager to run. Arnold decided to go for a ride before anything else interfered.

In the barn while he was saddling Black Shadow, Shoo Ann and Alice approached him and asked to go along.

"Sure. Did you invite Beth?" he asked.

"We did, but she declined," Shoo Ann replied.

While Shoo Ann and Alice saddled their horses, Arnold inspected Black Shadow for wounds and combed the tangles out of his mane and tail. The horse stood perfectly still while he was handled. Arnold murmured to him and wondered how much the horse understood.

The three riders started on their journey at a gallop. Before long, they slowed the horses to a trot and finally to a walk. Black Shadow displayed some of his stallion spirit and nuzzled both mares as if asking for some love and affection.

Alice had never seen this before, and she was curious.

"Will the horses actually have intercourse this afternoon while we are out riding?" she asked.

"No." Arnold answered. "Neither mare is in season."

"What does that mean," Alice asked.

"The mares have already been bred by a stallion and would not welcome sex again until after they have delivered their foals and completed nursing."

"They should be able to have intercourse more often than that," Alice commented.

"That is why I never wanted to be a mare," Shoo Ann declared. "I want to be able to have sex whenever I wanted to." Then she added, "like today, or right now, and again tomorrow. Am I making myself clear?"

"That is pretty clear," Arnold chuckled. "And it just might happen."

The three rode on even as it began to get cold. The temperature had been falling all day. Shoo Ann rode up beside Arnold.

"Has Beth talked to you about a new applicant to work on the ranch?"

"She has," he replied.

"I met him at the restaurant. His name was Mr. Willy Carr. He seems to be a nice guy. He is married with four children, two boys and two girls. They live on a small ranch about four miles north of Alamosa, which he inherited from his parents about 12 years ago. He also wanted to know why Jerry was terminated."

Arnold did not want to get involved in this discussion so he answered abruptly. "You will have to tell him that he needs to discuss this with Beth as she is in charge of hiring and firing the people who work on the ranch."

They turned around and headed back to the barn. Upon their arrival, all three dismounted and began brushing their horses down. Arnold noticed that he could see his own breath in the cold and when he looked at the girls, their cheeks glowed pink from riding into the wind. The girls and the horses all looked healthy to Arnold. Before going to the house, they gave their horses some grain and turned them into the pasture where they could graze and drink water from the tank.

In the kitchen, Shoo Ann approached Beth about her firing of Jerry. "Why did you fire Jerry?" Shoo Ann asked. "He was a good worker."

Arnold walked into the kitchen at just that moment. Beth looked to him for help answering.

"Shoo Ann. Sit down at the table and we will discuss it," Arnold said.

Beth gave the soup she was cooking another stir and turned the heat down so she could be a part of the discussion.

"What do you want to know?" asked Arnold, taking charge of the conversation.

"I only have one question, that being why was Jerry terminated," Shoo Ann repeated her question.

"Jerry was terminated because Beth had brought up the idea of starting a romantic relationship with Jerry. I seriously objected to this and asked Beth to terminate Jerry to avoid further temptation."

"Now I have another question. May I ask it?" Shoo Ann asked.

"Yes, Arnold answered. "Ask any question you have?"

"Why were you so sensitive about Beth having a romantic relationship with Jerry? They had not begun a relationship yet."

"Oh Shoo Ann, it is a long story and not one that I want to tell unless both you and Beth agree to avoid discussing it further with anyone and forever keep it confidential."

"I agree," Beth said.

"I agree," Shoo Ann said.

"Some of the story of my divorce in Oklahoma you already know. It cost me 12 years of grief and I spent a lot of money defending my reputation and property that I did not have at that time. My wife cheated on me with another man and that man hired lawyers to take my property away."

The two women did not take their eyes off him as he continued.

"If there is another such event in my life, I will simply walk away and never return. I started to walk away from Beth this time for fear she would have a relationship with Jerry if he stayed, but decided I could not leave her because my father taught me to 'always do the right thing.' I promised Beth I would help her with the ranch and always treat her right. I wanted to keep that promise."

Shoo Ann looked at Beth, who had tears in her eyes.

"Beth, did you commit to avoiding romantic relationships with anyone who comes to work at the ranch?"

"Yes, and I intend to keep my commitment," Beth replied. "For the record, there never was a romantic relationship between Jerry and me. I merely had to know the answer to the question. I asked, but I will never ask it again. Jerry was very upset. I was too. It didn't seem fair that he was fired for flirting when he did such a darn good job."

"Any more questions?" Arnold asked.

"I have one question for Shoo Ann," Beth said. "Do you have or plan to have an emotional or romantic relationship with either Arnold or me?"

"I already have an emotional and sexual relationship with both you and Arnold. I am attached to both of you and want this to continue forever. People who originate from Indonesia or China, like me, have a tendency to love each other unconditionally without reservation," Shoo Ann said looking from one to the other.

"Since neither one of you will want fire me for flirting or making love to you, and since I have no other questions, I suggest we get that soup in some bowls and eat. It is late."

Edward K. Mackendrik

CHAPTER 13

Early the next morning, Arnold woke craving a good, strong cup of coffee and time by himself. Beth lay tangled in the sheets still sound asleep beside him. He got out of bed, carefully so as not to wake her. He needed time alone to think. He followed the aroma of coffee to the kitchen where the pot stood on the stove.

"God bless Shoo Ann," he thought.

No one was around. He poured himself a steaming cup and took his coffee out to the barn where he leaned against the warm boards on the sunny side of the building and watched Black Shadow graze. The horse nickered a greeting but did not interrupt his breakfast to move closer to Arnold.

Arnold had been feeling content for weeks now, but the firing of Jerry because Beth had been eyeing the hired man as a possible bedmate unearthed ugly memories of his past marriage and brought back the anxiety and confusion he often wrestled with.

"To avoid the possibility of being hurt, I demanded that Beth fire Jerry," Arnold acknowledged to no one but himself, "and she did it.

Maybe I am feeling guilty. Jerry had been a good worker who really knew horses."

"Do I blame Beth for asking me if I would mind if she had sex with Jerry?" Arnold asked himself.

No. Not really, he thought. All she did was ask, but when I answered her, it came out harshly, "It would bother me very much," leaving us both feeling awkward and exposed.

At the time, all Arnold could think of was Beth having sex with Jerry in the barn, in the farmhouse, in their favorite spot by the spring, in their bed. He remembered the farmhand he had caught her with in their bed, the one who put his boots on backward and fell all over himself in his hasty naked retreat. He did not believe Beth could work around Jerry every day without being tempted to have sex with him, and then he, Arnold, would feel betrayed...again as he was by Charlene years ago.

He swore he would not ever again go through 12 years of grief over a woman who cheated on him. Instead, he would walk away. If Beth had opted to not terminate Jerry, he would have walked away, never again to be seen or associated with Beth. He knew he would have broken his vow to help Beth recover from her sex-change surgery and to help her oversee the ranch until she fully recovered. Anxiety swirl through his stomach as he contemplated how close he came to breaking that promise and the philosophy he lived by, "Always do the right thing." Because of this promise, Arnold could not merely walk away from Beth. He truly believed that Beth and he shared an unconditional love, one for the other.

His coffee and his hands had grown cold. He pushed away his depressing thoughts and walked back to the ranch house to prepare to interview the new hired hand, Willy Carr.

Mr. Carr arrived promptly at 10:00 AM, a check mark in his favor. He was a tall man, not thin, not fat, just big. His hands were tanned and rough with hard work. He seemed to be about 35 years old. His brown hair snuck out from under his cowboy hat and curled at his neck. His pointed boots were leather and well worn.

Beth and Arnold interviewed the candidate together. They confirmed that Willy had more than five years of experience with cattle and horses. He had a lifetime of experience. He was raised on the ranch he now lived on, a 1,000-acre ranch four miles north of Alameda, but the ranch did not provide the income he needed to support his wife and five children, three boys and two girls the youngest being five and the oldest eleven. He was planning to supplement the income from his own ranch by working for someone else.

Willy Carr had worked previously for two other ranchers in nearby counties, but they had decided to reduce their operating costs and had terminated his employment. He offered their names and address as references.

At 11:00 AM, they took a short break, leaving Willy sitting at the kitchen table with a cup of coffee while they went out on the porch to discuss the interview. Beth made the decision to hire Willy if his salary requirements were not excessive.

Arnold and Beth returned to the kitchen and poured themselves fresh cups of coffee.

"I'd like to hire you Mr. Carr," Beth said. "Will $600.00 a month for a thirty-hour week work for you."

"That will do fine Ms.," he agreed.

"When can you start?" Beth asked with a broad smile.

"Today is Friday, so I guess I can start on Monday."

"Wonderful Mr. Carr. That will be just fine," Beth said.

"I do prefer to be called Willy," Willy Carr noted.

"Willy it is then," laughed Beth.

"Do you have time right now for me to show you around the ranch?" Asked Arnold.

"Sure. I do. Thank you for the job Mr. and Mrs. Barkley."

"Arnold," said Arnold placing his hand on his chest.

"Beth," said Beth mimicking Arnold and placing her hand on her chest with a slight bow.

Neither mentioned that they were not married. As Arnold and Willy headed out the door, Arnold winked at Beth, threw her a kiss, and said, "See you later Hon."

Willy would ride Beth's horse Autumn Time. Arnold pointed out the saddle and tack she used where it hung on the wall and Willy saddled Autumn Time while Arnold saddled Black Shadow. They set out on their tour at a brisk trot.

The day had warmed slightly. As they rode Arnold pointed out some of the recently repaired fences and several six-month old calves that needed close observation. He explained their practice of using artificial insemination instead of purchasing a bull or two.

Willy was familiar with each item they discussed, and he asked, "What month do you plan to impregnate the cows this year?"

Arnold responded, "Probably in late April or May because I would like the new crop of calves to appear in early March."

Arnold explained their lion issue and pointed out the llamas they had purchased to provide some protection. He also pointed out the goat herd they had purchased to deal with weeds and undergrowth in the trees alongside the creek.

Willy agreed that these protective measures worked well and told Arnold that he would purchase three or four young goats if he wanted to sell some.

"The purchase will probably occur each year if you agree because my wife and children love goat meat."

Arnold laughed at that. "Goats do proliferate. It will be nice to have a way to thin the herd."

The two men, both large and tall in their saddles rode along the creek and counted the goats. They observed the male goat performing his function breeding with three female goats while they were counting them.

"I need to tell Beth to expect new goats in 150 days," Arnold noted, nodding at the active male. "Willy you can take up to 4 baby goats home with you when you want them."

I'll bring the boys and girls over with me tomorrow and they can look over the goats. Maybe they would like to make a couple of them pets."

They rode on in silence for several minutes, admiring the pastures and the view of the snow-covered mountains.

"Have you met Janell?" Willy asked Arnold.

"I have." Arnold answered.

"She is thinking of leasing her ranch, which includes 1,500 acres, to someone outside the family because she is not able to take proper care of it. She also told my wife, who is her sister, that she sold one mare and might sell a second one if she could get as much for the second one as she did the first one."

That information interested Arnold.

"That is good to know. I think it would be nice to have another quarter horse for you to use while you are working here. What do you think? Would you like me to purchase the horse from Janell?"

"That would be great," Willy replied.

"I'll check into it as well as into leasing Janell's ranch land."

Willy and Arnold returned from their tour and while they were rubbing down the horses, Willy mentioned that he was going to the restaurant for lunch.

"We might join you there," Arnold remarked. "I'll find out if Beth is hungry."

Willy drove off in his red pickup as Arnold entered the house.

"Why don't we go to the restaurant for lunch," Beth suggested from the kitchen when she heard the door close behind Arnold. "We can see if Alice and Shoo Ann want to go too."

"Sounds like a great idea." Arnold agreed. "Willy is headed there now. I told him we might join him."

Arnold's big truck was filled to the doors as he drove to the restaurant. Shoo Ann and Alice were squished into the seat between Arnold and Beth and tried to keep their legs out of Arnold's way when he shifted gears. Beth and Arnold both had their windows rolled down and hung an arm out each side to give the two in the middle more room. Arnold informed Beth over the sound of the wind and the motor and over the heads of the two Asian women of the possibility that Janell wanted to lease her ranch and sell another quarter horse.

"I think we should consider leasing her land and purchasing the quarter horse," Arnold hollered.

"Hmm. Yes. Good idea." Beth agreed.

"Yes. A great idea. More horses. More riding," Shoo Ann offered giggling and sticking her elbow into Alice's ribs. "You need more experience sister."

"Oh, you're a hoot!" Alice yelled back.

"A hoot. What is a hoot?" asked Shoo Ann.

"It means. You're so funny. Learn to speak American. Sister." Alice retorted.

Arnold laughed. "I'm glad all the ladies agree. I'll approach Janell about both ideas."

The four joined Willy at his table when they got to the restaurant. They had to pull some chairs from a nearby table as Arnold introduced Willy to Alice and Shoo Ann, telling him they helped around the ranch too.

Lunch was delicious and Arnold ate more than he should have, especially of the apple pie and ice cream he had for dessert.

As they lingered over the last of their lunch, Janell came in the door for her own lunch and to chat with whomever was available. Arnold waved her over and asked, "would you like to join us and discuss the sale of another quarter horse? And, Willy here tells me you want to lease out your ranch."

"Well I am interested in discussing both," Janell stated her hands on her hips as she surveyed the group eating, "but you have quite a crowd here and you are almost finished with lunch. How about you join me at my home this afternoon?"

"How about 2:00 PM?" Arnold asked.

"That will be fine," Janell agreed and moved on to a table near the kitchen where she could talk to Maggie as she ate.

Willy took the interruption as time to leave. He said he would see them all in the morning when he brought his children to see the goats.

As the remaining four finished eating, Beth was eyeing Janell. She asked Arnold what he thought she should offer Janell.

Arnold replied, "$.75 per acre per year and Janell can purchase any barb wire and fence posts that might be needed. We have not inspected the fences yet."

"That is not enough," Beth objected. "She should get $1.00 per acre. Her father received $1.00 an acre five or six years ago."

"Okay, $1.00 an acre it is and for the quarter horse, $200.00?"

"I must check my bank account before committing to spending all of that," Beth said.

"Have you used up your buffer money?"

"No, I forgot about it."

"What do you need to check then?"

Beth pinched him in the side and said "You. Wise guy."

Arnold dodged to avoid another pinch and said he was going to ride Black Shadow over to Janell's ranch, tour the fence lines and evaluate the remaining quarter horse mare to see if the purchase and lease were as good a deal as they sounded.

The four got up, paid their bill, complimented Maggie on her cooking and service and left the restaurant to pile into the truck.

An hour later, Arnold set off on Black Shadow for Janell's ranch. When he got there, he tied Black Shadow to a hitching post and knocked on the door of the large white ranch house. Janell opened the door immediately and stuck her head out.

"I'd like to look the property over. Do you want to go with me?" Arnold asked.

"No, you go ahead. I want to finish a project or two in my house but do come in when you have inspected everything, and we will talk."

"Where is the quarter horse you might sell?" Arnold asked.

"She is right over there. The sorrel in the pasture," Janell pointed to a coppery red mare grazing contentedly along the fence line East of the house.

Arnold rode Black Shadow along all the fences and through all the gates. He noticed there was plenty of water running quietly in the creek. The fences were in good shape, and the grass did not appear to be overgrazed, indicating Janell kept only a few cows and horses on the property, not enough to damage anything. He decided to offer her the $1.00 per acre, and Beth would maintain the fences provided Janell purchased the required barbed wire and fence posts.

When he returned from inspecting the fences and the quality of grass, he looked at the horse barn and the two other outbuildings. One was being used as a garage for an old truck and small tractor.

He dismounted near the sorrel mare and climbing the fence was happy to see that she was unafraid of approaching him when he whistled. He patted her neck and ran his hands over her legs. Her tail reached almost to the ground. Her main was full and her copper hair smooth over big quarter horse muscles.

He proceeded to the back door of the ranch house and knocked. Janell opened the door and invited him in for a cup of coffee. He saw that she had placed a tablet of paper on the table.

As soon as she poured two coffees and sat down across from him, she asked what price Beth was going to offer?

"What do you want for a year lease and the sorrel?" Arnold countered.

"Who is buying? Beth or you?" Janell asked.

"Beth," Arnold answered. "Me I'm just an Okie rambling around Colorado helping lady ranchers," he added with a grin.

"Hmm," Janell looked him over. "An Okie with a talent for numbers I understand. More than meets the eye, I'd say."

"Well speaking of numbers, Beth is prepared to offer $1.00 per acre per year and we repair the fence as long as you buy the barbed wire and posts. When do you want the lease to start?"

"Immediately," Janell said. "How much for the quarter horse?"

"The same as I paid for the last one, $200.00."

"You know that $1.00 an acre for a year for the lease tallies to $1,500.00 a year. Can Beth handle that?"

"Will you purchase the barbed wire and fence-post when they are needed?" Arnold asked.

"Yes, I will if you drink some more of my fresh coffee and don't rush off now that the deal is struck."

"Count on it." Arnold said. "Beth can handle the price." He lifted his cup to show her it was already empty.

CHAPTER 14

It was near suppertime when Arnold reported back to Beth that she was now leasing 1,500 acres of ranch land and the owner of another quarter horse. He poured himself a whiskey and raised a glass to her to see if she wanted a drink. She shook her head and picked up her cup of hot tea from a nearby table.

"I think we need to sit and discuss how they were going to handle the new work and additional responsibilities," Arnold suggested.

Beth sat down in a chair holding her tea. She took a sip before saying anything. "I am thrilled to have the additional acres, but it is not adjacent to my ranch, and I really have no idea how to proceed."

Arnold took a seat in the chair facing her across the coffee table and lifted his tired feet onto a footstool. He took a long sip of the Jack Daniels.

"It is not complicated," he mused. He took another sip of his drink and continued. "First it is a matter of being organized and able to make sound judgement decisions."

Beth stared at him. "Piece of cake," she said.

Arnold snorted.

"Second, you have to decide how many cows can the 1,500 acres handle without supplementing with hay."

Beth thought for a moment and sipped her tea. She stated at a painting over Arnold's head of a slickered cowboy on a powerful black horse driving cows through a heavy rain that looked cold.

"I have always tried to allocate 10 acres per cow with calf and monitor their growth and if necessary, add hay or baled grass. If there is a lot of grass, I rarely have to supplement with hay," Beth said. "Given we have 1,500 acres at Janell's, we should be able to accommodate 150 cows and their calves."

"I think you should assign Willy to care for the leased land and loan him the quarter horse you just purchased. Let him provide his own saddle and gear," Arnold said. "Willy and I will visit Janell and estimate the amount of hay that is in her barn. We can decide if we need to order additional hay, assuming you are going to put 150 head on there right away."

"Where am I expected to get the money to purchase more cows in addition to the land and the horse?" Beth asked.

"We need to look at the market. I will do that early tomorrow and then decide if it is a good or a bad time to buy cows with calves. If it is a good time, we can use part of the "rainy day fund" to make the purchase."

The next day, after analyzing cattle prices for young cows with calves, because conditions were dry in some areas of Colorado and all over Texas, Arnold saw that the price per head was down. Consulting with Beth and Willy, he decided to purchase 150 veterinarian approved young cows with calves.

"Beth do you want to call the Auction barn and get a quote, or do you want me to handle that?"

"I'd really like for us to do that together. If possible, we can both visit the auction barn tomorrow so I can learn how to do this."

On Monday morning when he reported for his first day of work, Beth and Arnold approached Willy with their idea of assigning him to the leased land as well as the original ranch work. He was pleased with the arrangement.

"Where are you intending to buy the 150 cows and calves?" Willy asked.

"Wherever we can get the best one's for the money," Arnold stated.

"I know of a ranch where they are going to sell their cows as soon as they can. However, they are trying to avoid the commission at the auction barn. Maybe you would like to visit the ranch and evaluate their herd," Willy suggested.

Beth, Willy, and Arnold drove over to the ranch that very morning since they had not started any jobs for the day.

When they talked to the ranch owner, they learned that indeed he did want to sell some cows without going through the auction barn and that the cows were pregnant and had been inspected and vaccinated by a veterinarian.

Arnold was quickly learning that Willy had very good cow judgement, and he was outstanding at estimating a cow's weight.

Willy, Beth, and Arnold estimated the cows averaged 800 pounds each. Avoiding the commissions from the auction barn would save them $20.00 for each cow. Because the cows were already vaccinated by the veterinarian they would save or avoid paying $40.00 per cow for his services, thus savings $7,000.00 total for the 150 cows.

Assuming they paid $.30 cents a pound for each cow weighing an average of 800 pounds, the purchase price would be $24,000.00.

Arnold turned, to Beth and asked, "Do you want to buy them?"

"Yes, if we have the money," Beth replied quietly.

"We have the money." Arnold assured her.

Arnold looked at Willy. The two men grinned at each other as if they had won the lottery. Arnold turned to the owner and said,

"We will buy your cows, Mr.—?"

"Franklin, Franklin Berger."

"Okay! Mr. Berger. Franklin. We will buy your cows for $24,000.00 provided you can provide the vaccination records."

"I have them," the Franklin said, "right here." He handed the papers to Arnold.

"How far is it from your ranch Franklin to the Janell ranch where we are going to put the cows?"

Franklin thought for a moment. "It is 15 miles."

"Do you have enough cowboys to drive them from your place to our place?" Asked Arnold.

"I do if you pay each cowboy, there are 10 of them, $100.00 each."

"When can you drive them over?" Arnold asked.

"In the morning, early." Franklin answered.

"How early?" Arnold asked.

"We will leave our ranch at 5:00 AM, and we will arrive by 4:00 PM." Franklin said.

"Excellent! I'll buy dinner for everyone and hand each cowboy a hundred-dollar bill."

Franklin's grin stretched across his whiskered face.

"I like your style Mr."

On the way back to the Beth Ranch, Arnold stopped by the restaurant and told Maggie she would have about 15 mouths to feed at 5:00 PM the next day.

Arnold could tell she was thrilled with the news, and even happier when he said he was paying.

Back in the truck he asked Beth if she wanted to eat at the restaurant with the rest of them.

Beth, seated in the middle seat between Arnold and Willie, turned to each man and smiled.

"You could not keep me away."

The next morning, Arnold was up well before sunrise. It was going to be a frosty morning. Beth already had the coffee on. The smell warmed and cheered the house. Arnold was convinced this was going to be a great day, and he did not want to miss one moment of it.

As soon as he ate breakfast, he climbed into his winter gear and went out to saddle up Black Shadow. He saddled Autumn Time too. He sat on Black Shadow thinking of his farm in Oklahoma and of his father and Mother. He wished they could see the smile on his face. He knew his smile would convince them that their wayward son was trying to do the right thing and God was smiling on him.

Beth exited the house intending to saddle Autumn Time. She found her horse standing with her saddle already where it belonged. In the yard, she walked her beautiful quarter horse close beside Black Shadow, stood in the stirrups, and gave Arnold one of the best kisses she could muster.

"Sweetheart, life is good!" Arnold laughed.

Beth looked at Arnold and said "Arnold, I don't know where great men come from or how they are made, but if I could copy your parent's recipe, I surely would be a rich woman. Every day you make me so happy."

Just then, Willy arrived for work. He rode up on the new sorrel and informed Arnold that he had made a list of priority projects for him to undertake on each place, making the "Beth Ranch" the highest priority and the "Janell Ranch" the second.

"Will you both review my list and give me some feedback?"

Arnold reached over from where he sat on Black Shadow and accepted Willy's list. He smiled at Beth, "See, I told you sweetheart. Today is a good day."

Beth laughed and Willy looked at them a little confused.

"You need to look at page 22," said Willy.

Arnold quickly turned to page 22 and to his surprise, it was there in black and white. The cows were artificially inseminated using sperm from a Hereford Sire from the King Ranch in Texas on August 15, 1958. Arnold then calculated the expected date for the cows to begin delivering calves as April 15, 1959.

"Ah Ha," he said. "The calves are due the same day the IRS lowers the boom on everybody!"

Laughing happily, they rode out of the ranch yard toward Janell's ranch. Arnold could tell Beth was a proud and happy lady, and he was pleased.

After a few minutes, Beth rode Autumn Time up beside Black Shadow and maneuvered her very close to big stallion. Her stirrups touched Arnold's. He thought he was getting another kiss and leaned in her direction. She reached across the space between them, grabbed a handful of Arnold's coat, leaned toward him, and whispered in his ear, "Arnold, I wish I could tell you I was pregnant with our child."

She retreated immediately and sat straight in her saddle, reining Autumn Time away a couple of feet. He could see that tears were running down her cold cheeks.

What a beautiful person she is, he thought.

"Beth, so do I."

Without haste, Arnold, Beth, and Willy rode their horse over to the Janell Ranch where they began to visualize the arrival of 150 calves. When they got there, Beth and Arnold proceeded to count hay bales and determine how many more bales they would need. They were pleasantly surprised to see that they had enough hay already.

Sitting in their saddles waiting, they realized they really did not have anything to do yet. The cows would not arrive for several hours, so the three of them decided to ride over to Maggie's for a late breakfast. They all needed coffee and food because they had been so excited to get started, they had forgotten to eat breakfast earlier. This gave them the opportunity to discuss menu options for the coming evening.

As always, Maggie had everything under control and presented her plan for steak, potatoes, carrots, a salad, fresh baked buttered rolls, and plenty of coffee and iced tea to drink. All they needed to do was eat, so they ordered big breakfasts and lingered at the table drinking coffee and talking to other patrons of the restaurant as they came in.

Maggie came over and told Arnold that he had a call from Charlie Anderson on the restaurant phone.

Arnold got up, picked up the phone and listened with amazement as Charlie said, "I ran into the oil and gas Landman and he has a crew of oil executives and prospectors with him evaluating the latest two sections of land for the purpose of leasing them. They are willing to offer $40.00 per acre for 320 acres or $12,800.00 in a one-time contract lasting for 20 years."

Arnold was silent so Charlie continued. "While that sounds good, the great news is that they intend to expand current drilling activity to include the two sections. He said their projected date to begin drilling is only 3 or 4 months from today."

Arnold was still silent, so Charlie took a breath and continued. "The Landman expressed the intent to contact you within a few days. He projects wells will be drilled on each quarter, and he said, there would be about 8 per quarter. He also calculated that there would be 64 wells that would produce about the same as the current wells ($300.00 per month each x 64 wells), $19,200.00 per month, approximately $230,000.00 annually. "

Beth could see Arnold standing next to the phone on the wall of the restaurant. He stood so still she thought he was frozen. He was not saying anything, just looking at the receiver.

"Boss are you still there?" asked Charlie.

CHAPTER 15

Arnold made reservations for another flight to Oklahoma with the return date open because he wanted to see the oil well drilling plans for his land and how construction of his home was progressing. He wanted to see the house as it went up. Beth was extremely occupied with her project with the nuns to build a school and home for girls in Alamosa. She had at first wanted to go with him to Oklahoma, but remembered she had five meetings schedule during the time he planned to be gone. She had been elected President of the Alamosa Education and Advancement Home for Homeless Ladies, as the home and school was now called, and she was pleased, but she was busier than she had planned to be, but for a great cause.

So, Arnold flew to Oklahoma alone once again. The closer the plane came to touch down at the Oklahoma City Airport, the happier Arnold was to be home in Oklahoma. His rental car was not available, so the Avis people upgraded him to a Cadillac. He was pleased and as he drove out of the parking lot in the Cadillac, he thought it ironic that he had departed Oklahoma in a beat up pickup and now arrived back in a Caddy.

"Not bad for an Okie," he said to the broad sparkling windshield.

He rented a motel room in El Reno, leaving his date of departure open. "Carli" the young redhead at the desk got flustered trying to understand how to record his coming and going in the register.

"Sweetheart just go along with the flow," he advised, leaning over the counter, and snagging the key to his room. "if anyone gets on your case, tell them to see me as you have done nothing except try to accommodate a customer without compromising your principles."

As Arnold walked away from the reception desk, Carli recovered some of her aplomb.

"Well Mr. Barkley perhaps I will compromise a bit more next time," she said with a grin.

Arnold turned around and grinned back. He reached out and handed her his personal card with his home phone number on it and said, "You know where I'm at. Call me."

He walked away hoping she would call.

When Arnold was settled in his room, he called Charlie Anderson and they agreed to meet right away at Charlie's office. Upon his arrival, Arnold noticed a pile of new lumber adjacent the cattle pens.

Something is always going on at this farm, he thought.

Once inside Charlie's office, Charlie told him that Alex would arrive soon.

"Why don't we enjoy a cup of good coffee while we wait for her?" Charlie asked.

Arnold asked him about the lumber pile to fill time.

"I am replacing some of the boards on the cattle pens. If I have some left over from that, I was thinking of adding a couple of pens to be used when needed. I might even really go crazy and add a chute for loading and unloading livestock."

"How much will that cost?" Arnold asked.

"I estimate that the two pens and a chute would cost $1,850.00 in lumber."

"Go ahead and plan to make the chute and extra pens and take the bill to Darrell to be paid," Arnold suggested.

Charlie's grinned stretched across his face. "That would be great. Thank you I'll do that."

Alex arrived. Her brown hair was pulled back in a ponytail as usual and she was dressed for ranch work in jeans and a flannel shirt. A heavy winter coat hung over her arm.

"Hi Alex. You remember Arnold Barkley don't you?" Charlie asked as he greeted Alex.

"I do," said Alex and stuck her hand out to shake Arnold's hand as he rose from one of the chairs in front of Charlie's desk.

"I want to update both of you on what is going on," said Charlie, "to make sure we are all on the same page. I've converted all cultivated land to grass and coordinated with the ASCS in El Reno. They approved all of it with the caveat that we will not graze the new grass for two years. We also agreed to add fertilizer each year. There were no other restrictions."

He glanced from Arnold to Alex before he continued.

"Alex has assumed responsibility for monitoring the status of all the land owned by you, Arnold, and managed by me. Her hours are from either 6:00 or 7:30 AM daily to 7:00 or 7:30 PM daily, and she is permitted to attend school functions as needed to support her daughters."

"Also," he looked up and nodded at Arnold, "I have increased her salary to $15.00 per hour per your request."

Alex gave each man a radiant smile at that news.

"Next, I want to tell you that I plan to retain heifers born to the current herd and sell bulls or make steers out of them and then sell them. This is in preparation for adding approximately eighty head of cows to my normal year-round everyday breeding stock. I also plan to change to artificial insemination starting this spring. Most of the current stock will be ready by March.

If you have any questions, Arnold, refer them to Alex. She has the most up to date on the details of every part of the operation.

The 4H ladies are a total success and won several prizes at the latest fair competitions," said Charlie. "I want to confirm with you, Arnold, that you were still offering a $100.00 prize for those individuals who won prizes at the fair."

"I am." Arnold confirmed.

"Eight ladies won prizes. Can I up that to ten so no one is left out?"

"I can provide $100.00 for each of the ten," Arnold agreed.

Charlie whooped and jumped up from his chair with his fists raised in victory. "Wonderful!" he all but shouted.

Arnold laughed and thought it was worth the extra cost just to see Charlie so happy. Arnold could tell Charlie was enjoying his work helping the 4H ladies.

Alex spoke up then too. She had tears in her eyes as she watched Charlie practically dance a jig with joy.

"I am so grateful too. I am thankful for my job and for the attention my daughters are receiving. I am so happy to see their interest in raising calves. Their grades have improved from an average "C" to an average "A" too. My daughters wanted me to thank you for my job. For the first time this school year, they have new clothes and shoes, and they are thankful ladies."

Arnold said, "Alex, why don't you show me the new properties again, and we can drop in on the lady that did not want to move out of her house when she sold it to us."

Alex agreed. They put on their coats and waved to Charlie as they pulled away from his office in Alex's truck. They drove west to tour of the two added sections of land. Arnold noticed that Alex seemed to always work in a timely and productive manner.

As they drove, Arnold asked, "Have your finances improved Alex?"

"Yes," she said as she turned the wheel to make a wide turn into the yard of the house where Susan lived. Susan was the older woman who had stayed in her home after Arnold bought it.

"They definitely have and will continue to improve with my new pay raise."

The two knocked on the old woman's door and were invited in for coffee. Arnold was relieved to see that Susan was doing fine in her own unique way. After the visit, they returned to Charlie's office and Alex took leave of Arnold in the parking lot, dropping him off at his big Cadillac.

"Thanks Alex, my plans for the evening are to eat, relax and prepare for my mid-morning meetings."

"Well, my plans include two young squirrelly girls, their chores, and ballet practice," admitted Alex. "Dinner and sleep will be squeezed in there somewhere."

Back in his motel room, Arnold checked the weather forecast and was pleased to hear there were no storms for the area.

His scheduled meeting with Darrell the next morning was fruitful and reflected a system of handling money that proved to be efficient and accurate. Oil and gas production continued to astound even senior oil company executives and exceeded all predictions. Records maintained at the bank seemed to accurately reflect investment receipts documented by D, D, and C Accounting.

Darrell, who Arnold had known for 25 years expressed relief that Arnold now had confidence in his bank. "I knew you had doubts about this new system because of your frequent questions about account balances. I want to assure you that I am committed to accuracy, timeliness, and full disclosure on demand."

Satisfied that his accounts were in good honest hands, Arnold departed the bank and headed for the school gymnasium for his meeting with Betty and the 4H group.

Betty had arranged for the 4H group to brief him on their program. Charlie Anderson, as an associate member also attended the meeting. Betty introduced the girls, one at a time, and complimented each one on their achievements, especially those winning at the local fair. They each gave a quick speech explaining how they won their prizes, and Betty made presentations of $100.00 to each participant.

There were laughs and giggles and words of appreciation from the young ladies. Happy parents sat in the bleachers. Arnold could not help but feel good about everything.

Betty reported the girls were going to assist Charlie in the construction of the additional pens and chute.

"This will be a challenge for them because they have no carpentry experience. With Charlie's help, and the help of the shop teacher, and with the help of other assistants from the school, we are confident the girls will succeed and learn a lot. Now, the girls need to return to school for their next classes."

As the chattering girls departed, Arnold stopped each of them. He shook their small hands and told them he was proud of their work and that they should be proud of their achievements.

After the girls left for class and the parents left for home or work, Betty, Arnold, and Charlie walked together to the parking lot.

"I am so pleased with every member and look forward to more experiences in the near future, including the State Fair, which is scheduled for late next September," Betty said.

"How are you doing Betty with the duplex and with your schedule of teaching school and working with the 4H members?" Arnold asked.

"I am happy and busy," she said. "Alex is doing so well. Thank you for getting her that job. She has progressed so fast in that. I apologize that I don't have time to entertain you two gentlemen like a true Okie woman should," Betty grinned. "I need to depart for my next class too. I'll give you a call later Arnold if that is okay."

"Ah yes. It is the middle of the day isn't it. I have to meet with my accountants," Arnold said and kissed her gently on one warm tanned cheek. Charlie gave her a hug and they all parted ways.

Arriving at the offices of D, D, and C, Arnold was shown to a conference room where Linda was set up to summarize the activities that had occurred since Arnold had retained their services. There were 5 other accountants and executives in the room. Linda gave him a wave as he entered the room.

"Okay everyone, Arnold Barkley is here. Let's get started," Linda announced.

Speaking directly to Arnold, she began. "The current $41 million, will be added to the $22 million originally transferred plus the earnings of $1 million will bring you up to date with a total of $64 million. Calculating an estimated return of 3% without further additional revenue for the following year you can expect to tell the IRS that your earnings from now to the end of the year will be approximately $ 19,200.00."

Taking a breath, Linda quirked her lips and ended her summary with, "What I am saying, Mr. Barkley is you can now buy yourself a cup of coffee and not worry about paying for it."

Everyone around the conference table enjoyed a good laugh.

Arnold wanted to enjoy the moment and asked if he could borrow Linda for a few moments while he estimated future oil and gas earnings.

The executives and Linda agreed, and Linda led him to her office where together they calculated an estimate of his oil and gas revenue for the year. They came up with $1,200,000 over 12 months.

Sticking his head back in the conference room as Linda walked him back through the offices, he thanked D, D, and C and for their assistance and asked if anyone wanted lunch. Everyone except Linda had appointments. They quickly suggested Linda take him to lunch and they would pick up the tab.

Arnold and Linda headed to a nearby steakhouse to celebrate on D, D, and C's tab.

Over cocktails before lunch, Linda told Arnold that she had become engaged to a young man and they planned to get married within a month or two, depending on Linda's work schedule.

Arnold was sincerely happy for her.

After lunch, curious, Linda asked as he drove her back to her office, "Are you disappointed that I am engaged to get married? I mean given our history."

"I am somewhat disappointed because you and I have become true friends, and I could see us moving further in a relationship. However, since you are engaged, we must enhance our relationship in ways that do not encourage us to spend time alone with each other. To be true and candid, if you were not planning to get married and had not already pledged your commitment to your husband to-be, I would be after you in the same manner as I was before I knew of your plans. You are one beautiful and smart woman. Who knows what the future holds? Had we conducted ourselves differently these last few months, things might be different for us today."

Arnold paused and looked over at Linda. Tears were spilling from her eyes. He bit down hard on his lip to keep tears from forming in his eyes too.

"But, we didn't, and here we are saying good-bye."

"Can you drive around a bit while I pull myself together?" Linda asked.

She took a shaky breath, "Arnold, I did not know you thought that way about me and I am sad. Now that I have decided though, I will stay with it."

Arnold drove around in silence for ten minutes or so until Linda said, "Now you can drop me off at the office. However, I will not say good-bye, ever. Please enjoy your visit to Oklahoma."

Arnold departed for Robert's office. Robert was waiting for him and said as soon as Arnold walked in the door, "I've made a fresh pot of coffee," and waved him into his office.

"You are okay, apparently it is not true what everybody says about you," Arnold joked.

The two old friends chuckled a little at the old joke that should be dropped. Robert was as pleasant as ever. They discussed the real estate market for an hour before Robert asked about Arnold's future plans.

"My investments are very productive, Arnold admitted. I could be persuaded to purchase more land if it is adjacent to the other sections I own. Because of the oil and gas activity around here, the price of land, especially that retaining mineral rights, has skyrocketed, and those last properties you found for me, have tripled in price."

"Your real estate holdings are now worth three times the price you paid for them," Robert agreed.

"What are the prices of the adjacent land?" Arnold asked.

"Ironically, their prices have not increased and may not ever increase because the oil companies have not expressed any intent to lease that land. In fact, they have refused to lease any of it."

"For the purpose of discussion, how much would I have to pay for the four sections on the south side of the four sections I currently own? Arnold asked.

"Only three days ago I listed those four sections for sale at a price of $120,000.00 each, or $30,000.00 per quarter," replied Robert.

"I need to make a phone call," Arnold said. "May I use your phone?"

"Certainly, I'll step away and give you some privacy," Robert replied.

Arnold dialed Charlie Anderson and asked him if he was interested in managing an additional four sections of land immediately south of the land he currently manages.

"I would be interested if the sections are adjacent to the land I am already managing."

Arnold said, "They are."

"I am definitely interested then and would do it on the same terms as their current deal."

Arnold said, "Okay then," and hung up the phone.

Calling to Robert, he said, "Prepare contracts for me to sign. You have made a sale. I want to purchase the four sections that are adjacent to mine. I will gamble on the decision made by the oil and gas company. They are mistaken and are using their strategy to rob the local people from making good money. Bring them on and we will see who robs who."

Robert took over from there as he handed his secretary the legal descriptions of each piece of property.

"Make three contracts, one for each section of land, then on the fourth section, we will need two contracts one for the south two quarters and one for the north two quarters. They are owned by different parties."

Within 20 minutes, Robert's secretary (she was introduced to Arnold as Phyllis) produced error-free contracts ready for signature.

Arnold reviewed each one as she completed it and signed each contract. As he was signing the fourth and fifth contracts Robert asked if he would mind if Charlene followed up on the contracts as he himself needed to leave for Dallas. He should have left that morning but waited to discuss these properties with Arnold.

Arnold said that he did not mind at all.

Robert called Charlene, explained the situation, and told Arnold that Charlene was on her way; then said, "I have contacted the owners, and they will be here within a few minutes to sign as they know rental agreements are already due for signing and they have been waiting to see if they could get a buyer."

Charlene arrived at the real estate office soon after Robert left. She hugged Arnold and they chatted with Phyllis until the owners arrived in a noisy happy group. Once all the signatures were in place, Phyllis made copies of the signed contracts for Arnold and he went on his way.

He stopped by Charlies' office once again, and Charlie wanted to know when he would take possession of his latest purchase?

"The day after closing, which will be in two weeks," Arnold said.

Alex arrived in the office and Arnold asked Charlie if the three of them could tour the new 4 parcels of land. Charlie squeezed between Arnold and Alex and they bounce around the new land in Alex's truck.

As she looked over the expanse of land Arnold now owned and her employer now managed, Alex whispered. "That is what security looks like."

CHAPTER 16

Arnold stopped at the restaurant in El Reno and ate dinner alone. It was about 7:30 PM when he arrived at the motel. He called Beth and found out that even though he had left Willy, Beth, and Shoo Ann to settle the new herd in at Janell's ranch, everything had gone well.

A light snow was falling. Thanksgiving Day was a week away. Fully clothed, he lay in his bed, exhausted from the activities of the day. Even though the day had been full of good news and good purchases, worries ran through his head. First among his concerns was Alex. She is trying to raise two young girls on a salary of $15.00 per hour and living in a house that needs significant repairs, he thought. Then there was Susan, an elderly lady in the country alone with few visitors, eating alone with nothing to listen to but the cold wind and the creaking of the old house, aging with just her imagination to stir the stillness. He was concerned about Betty too. She worked every day to ensure 10 young girls have a chance to learn about life through the 4-H club. Betty is a vibrant woman, widowed and active in the community, but wanting companionship, a teammate, and a better life. Finally, there is Charlene, his own ex-wife, a beautiful woman, more attractive than most women, divorced and remarried and divorced again, now living in an open marriage, one that permits sexual relationships outside of the marriage. He thought of Beth and Brenda, the two women he felt the most emotionally tied to.

He wondered what his parents would have thought of all the women in his life.

I'm sure they would have asked, "What happened to you and the values you were raised with? You sleep around with so many women. You want the women to be faithful to you, but you are not faithful to them. Don't you remember that one man should be with one woman, from the beginning to the end, forever loyal and true until death do you part?"

"Yes, mother and father. I remember." he imagined himself answering. "These women and I have lost our way in life. We may never be able to find our way home."

For a few minutes he felt short of breath, smothered, hot, and anxious. A voice in his head asked, "Arnold when are you going to make a decision to return to Calumet, Oklahoma and live in your home that is being built right now? When Arnold, When? And, who are you bringing home to live with you?"

At that very moment, someone knocked on the motel room door. Arnold sprang up, shocked and alarmed. Without hesitation, he jerked open the door and stuck his head out, looking right into the startled eyes of Alex.

Alex jumped back with a tiny scream.

Once their breath returned, they both laughed and before they knew it, they were hugging as if they were afraid someone would rip them away from each other.

Alex stepped back first and her dark eyes surveyed the disheveled man before her.

"Are you okay Arnold?" she asked. "You are wild eyed and dripping sweat. Do you feel okay?"

Arnold stepped back and motioned Alex into the room. He looked in the mirror and realized he looked awful and felt awful. He looked at his watch and noticed it was 11:35 PM. Where had the time gone? He sat down on the foot of the bed, trying to collect himself.

"I must have fallen asleep and was dreaming," he guessed.

Alex sat down next to him and looked into his confused eyes. She put one arm around him in a hug and gave him a gentle kiss on the lips that surprised him, surprised both of them, and brought Arnold back to life. He called room service and ordered two drinks then he quickly changed his order to one Jack Daniels and ginger ale and one hot chocolate.

Arnold went into the bathroom to straighten up a bit and wash his face. When he came out the drinks arrived. Alex took the drinks from the waiter. She looked the drinks over with one eye closed.

"Arnold, which drink is mine?" she asked.

She grinned at her own joke and handed the Jack Daniels to him and sitting down on the only chair in the room took a sip of her hot chocolate.

It hit him then, like a ton of bricks, he loved Alex. This was the Alex he had come to love and had not told anyone of his feelings, not even himself. Immediately, he asked Alex, "Who is staying with the girls?"

"Charlie Anderson," she replied. "He is helping me in more ways than one can ever know. He will tell you more tomorrow. I came to see you because earlier today you said you would call me, and you did not. You have always called me when you said you would Arnold. Hear me now, I was worried about you. That is the truth."

Arnold sat on the side of the bed and recalled that he had promised to call Alex. "Ah, yes. I was going to call you because I was worried about you and your two daughters. I was even dreaming about that. As you can see, I am fine, and you are fine too it seems."

"I am, and you are looking better now."

Alex finished her chocolate in a slurp. They laughed at each other as Alex put on her winter coat. Then, she hugged him a second time, gave him a chaste kiss on the cheek, and opened the motel door.

"I can't believe you came looking because you were worried about me." Arnold said shaking his head. "No one has ever done that before. Have breakfast with me at the café in Calumet?" Arnold asked.

"What time?"

"You are the working woman with children. What time do you want to meet?"

"Either 5:00 AM or 8:30 AM. I have work to do between those time and after."

"8:30 AM works for me," Arnold said.

"Sounds Good. Sleep tight Mr. Barkley." Alex stepped out and climbed into her old reliable truck waving at him as she backed out of the parking lot and returned to her home and her daughters.

Arnold closed the door and fell back on the bed. He could hear the truck as she drove off. He thought, "God, there are some very good people in this world who have the values his parents told him about and taught him to live by. How could I have missed this? Am I blind to goodness? Do I see only the ugliness that exists? Please God, help me to see these values in others. Guide me."

He rose from the bed, undressed for bed this time, and crawled under the covers. He went to sleep immediately.

It was 7:30 AM when he woke. He took a shower and got ready for his day. He did not want to miss his breakfast appointment, so he left for the restaurant at 8:00 AM.

He wanted to see Alex. Something about her engaged his brain, motivated him to do what is right. He wanted to fully connect with Alex, to see things as she did. Her goodness was attractive. He wanted to be able to trust. He was starting to realize that he craved intimacy on more than a physical level. He wanted to escape from the carnal world he had come to be living in. He wanted a friend.

When he entered the café, it was 8:30 and he was starving. Alex was seated, reading the paper with a cup of coffee steaming in front of her.

"Good morning. Alex. How are you doing this morning?" He asked. "How are your daughters?"

"Everything is fine, and everyone is fine." Alex replied.

After Arnold was served coffee, and they had both ordered food, he asked if she was pleased with the addition of land or if it was just added work to her.

"I am very happy to have the security of more work, but I am concerned about getting everything accomplished."

"What is your workday like?" He asked and took a sip of coffee.

"Well, I start my work after I get the girls off to school. That is usually 7:15 AM when the girls leave to catch the bus. I start immediate and seldom stop before 4 or sometimes 5:00 PM. I check all the fences on your property and on Charlie's to see if they or the gates need repair. If they do, I report it back to Charlie over the two-way radio and document the location and the repair needed. I also check on work that is being done by contractors, and after work is done, I check to make sure it is completed correctly and sign off on invoices. Last, I keep a record of the quality of the work in case we want to use the contractor again or say Adios."

Alex stopped talking when their breakfast arrived and sipped her coffee.

Arnold looked at his plate as he admitted, "I think about you Alex and worry about you."

"Everyone knows you're a kind man Arnold. I really only have one worry. I worry about my house now that winter is approaching. It is difficult to keep warm."

"Why is that?" he asked.

"The bedrooms are not well insulated, and the cold wind comes in around the windows. The temperature is difficult to raise regardless of the way I set the thermostat."

"How much rent do you pay for this house?" he asked.

"$150.00 plus I pay all the utilities. They add up fast in the wintertime. Sometimes they reach $700.00."

"Do you want to move to another and better house?"

"I tried to find a way to do that last year, couldn't swing it. It looks like the same will be true this year," she replied, her voice dropping off as she finished. Her shoulders slumped a little as she turned back to her pancakes.

"If you found a house, how would you physically move your possessions?" Arnold asked.

"The 4-H group promised to move me if I get the chance." She smiled.

"How are your daughters?"

"They are doing great, no trouble, and their grades have improved from last year."

"I know I have been asking you questions like this was a game of 20 questions, but I want to ask one more then I have to leave for an appointment," Arnold said.

"What is it that you most want right now. What do you think about needing every day?" Arnold asked, looking straight into Alex's eyes.

"A good husband," Alex replied honestly, holding his gaze. "I miss being married and sharing the joys and burdens of life with someone."

Arnold nodded.

The waitress brought the check, and he paid it. He and Alex walked out to the parking lot together. He was headed out to his new house to talk to the contractor. House construction was a little slower in the winter, but it was still progressing.

"I check on your house every day." Alex said as she reached her truck and opened the door.

Arnold unlocked the door of his rental car and gave her a pleased smile. "Thank you, Alex. That is above and beyond your duty."

Reaching the farm and his new home, Arnold sat looking at it and remembering his plight when he left Oklahoma in July of 1956. He had been obsessed with not knowing who he was, what he was doing or what he was about. Now, he knew who he was, and he had found a passion in helping others who could not help themselves.

Getting out of his car, he walked around the framed shell of the house that was going up. The ground had frozen into ruts. The smell of fresh lumber and sawdust surrounded him. He waved to the contractor.

"Mr. Ellis. How are you?"

"Doin' fine Mr. Barkley. Are you here to look around?"

Arnold and Ellis toured the work and Arnold looked out of the framed rectangles where windows would be. All the land he could see was now his.

Ellis told him that the house was scheduled to be completed in two months, and he would ask the Canadian County Housing Inspectors to perform an occupancy permit inspection then. After that, Arnold could move in.

Arnold was sitting in his car again when he saw Alex's truck bumping up the road.

He got out of the car and greeted her with a warm hug. They stood beside the car and gazed at his house.

"It will be ready in two months," Arnold told her.

"I bet you feel so happy you can just crow." Alex said and gave a crow of her own into the wind.

"Alex. I wish I could marry you and give you that husband you want so much?" Arnold said.

Alex blinked in the bright sunlight. She grinned widely. "Shall I crow again? Will that help you decide?"

She looked at him like she was waiting to start crowing. Arnold stared at her then burst out laughing.

"I guess friend for life will have to do. I can't have you crowing all over the place. But, seriously, friends help friends. Let's get out of the cold and over to my bank and resolve some of your current financial issues. Alex. I have money. You need money."

Alex followed Arnold to the bank in her truck. In the parking lot, she grabbed Arnold arm and turned him around to face her.

"Are you sure? Arnold?" She asked. "I can't believe this is happening. I am so grateful."

"Believe it, Honey. Sometimes, I actually know what I'm doing." Arnold laughed and opened the door for her.

Inside, Arnold withdrew $5,000.00 and gave it to Alex right there. He asked if she had an account at the bank. She replied in the affirmative.

Off to the side, he asked Robert, the banker, to confidentially deposit $1,000.00 from his account into her account each month until he issued a stop order. The banker got the papers out and Arnold signed them.

"Let's go back to the farm with some wine and celebrate." Arnold suggested.

They bought a bottle of wine at a nearby liquor store.

"Let's take the truck. It can get around better on the back roads," Alex offered.

Together, they took her truck back out to the farm and drove on past the house towards the pond. There they sat on the frozen grass and watched the sun slowly lower in the west. Arnold told her about all his favorite places on the farm when he was a boy, and she vowed to visit each one of them while he was back in Colorado.

"I'm still a little stunned by your generosity," she sighed.

"How about dinner?" Arnold asked. "Let's go pick up Charlie and the girls and head to a restaurant."

Over burgers and steaks, Charlie told Arnold how important Alex was to his organization.

"I want her to be happy and safe," Charlie said. "The lady who was renting my personal home in Calumet has decided to relocate out of state and live next to her own children, and I want to know if Alex would like to move into my home."

"How much rent would I have to pay each month?" Alex asked.

"Since you work for me, there will be no rent or utility costs. I will pay it all," stated Charlie.

"You are so kind and generous. I can't believe this day. Thank you, Charlie. I'd love to live in your house."

Charlie noticed Alex had hardly touched her meal.

"I think you had better get to eating or you will run out of time. I'm already thinking about dessert."

"When can Alex move into your house?" Arnold asked.

"Next Tuesday. I'll bring her the keys," Charlie said.

"How are you going to manage the move? These two squirts won't be much help?" Charlie asked, pointing at the giggling girls who were busy swiping fried potatoes off Arnold's plate when he wasn't paying attention.

"Girls! Stop that. Arnold will go hungry," Alex cried.

She turned from the girls to Charlie. "The 4-H ladies and their husbands and sons will help me. They already told me so. They knew I was in need of a new house."

Arnold paid the check. After dessert, the girls climbed into the truck between Arnold and Alex, while Alex returned Arnold to the rental car they had left in the liquor store parking lot. She got out while he unlocked the car.

She asked, "When are we going to see you again?"

"The house will be done in two months. I'll be back in a month." He said and kissed her chastely on the forehead. "Be careful now."

Leaving Oklahoma was always difficult for Arnold, but leaving this time was excruciating. Before the plane left the ground, he was already planning his next trip.

A song made popular by Mr. Tony Bennett kept running through his head," I lost my heart in San Francisco."

He sang to himself, "I left my heart in Oklahoma, out on the range, it calls to me— but not for looong."

CHAPTER 17

As Arnold arrived in Pueblo, he felt anxious to get home.

His feelings were so contradictory, he thought. One minute I'm was longing for Oklahoma. The next I'm longing for the mixed-up family at the Beth Ranch. I know I left Beth and Willy with a lot of ranch work to take care of but the work is routine stuff and should not have been a problem.

As he drove into the yard of the Beth Ranch, Arnold realized how beautiful it was and how he was becoming attached to it. He loved the work of running a ranch. He walked to the barn, as was his custom when he returned, and brushed Black Shadow thoroughly. He stayed a while longer to watch the stallion strut around the corral as if he owned it. He wondered briefly why Black Shadow was so animated until he saw that Willy's mare was in the corral with Black Shadow because Willy was using the truck to get around the ranch that day. He remembered that Janell had not been able to recall the date of her mating, or if she had been bred at all. When they bought the mare, it had made no difference to them.

No wonder Black Shadow was in such a great mood, Arnold thought. Willy's mare, her name yet unknown to Arnold, was coming into heat and beginning to attract the big black stallion. Her behavior was that of a teaser and not one of being completely convinced the time was right.

Willy drove up and greeted Arnold. The truck window was open, and Willy's elbow was sticking out. Willy saw Arnold was eyeing Black Shadow and the mare.

"By my calculations, it might occur in 3 to 4 days," Willy called out.

"Good. Just in time for Shoo Ann and Alice to experience the miracle of a stallion and a mare mating," Arnold called back.

Willy chuckled at that.

"Did everything go alright while I was gone, Willy?" Arnold asked walking over to stand by the door of the work truck.

"Everything went fine. Shoo Ann seems to enjoy her newly assigned functions as watchdog. She alerted me to problems when she found them. She doesn't always know how to fix them, but she knows that you and I can fix things if we know about them."

"I knew she could do it," Arnold said as he straightened away from the truck.

"Good day now," Willy said and pulled away.

Arnold stayed out a while longer, enjoying the wintery sunshine and its surprising warmth.

Shoo Ann rode up on Sweetheart as he was idling in the sunshine.

"Hey Boss. You are looking good." She looked him over from up on her horse.

"You are looking good yourself," Arnold responded.

"Well, we need to do something more than looking. Follow me," Shoo Ann said as she swung down off Sweetheart and led her into the barn. Arnold followed.

In the barn she put her horse in her stall where a flake of hay was waiting for her and the water tank was full. Shoo Ann latched the stall, reached for a red blanket hanging from a post and spread it out on a level plane of stacked hay.

She turned to Arnold and began to unbutton her coat and dropped it on a hay bale. Then she unbuttoned her work shirt. When it was hanging loosely, she pitched her hat into the general area of the hay and winked at him.

Arnold was speechless and Shoo Ann's petite beauty was revealed. She pulled off her shirt and then pulled her undershirt over her head and kicked off her boots, affording him glimpses of her tiny breasts as she moved. She undid her hair from its ponytail.

"Don't just stand there in your work suit," Shoo Ann said with a smile.

Arnold gave a start, not looking away from the beautiful Asian lady and shrugged out of his coat, not caring where it landed on the floor of the barn. He began unbuttoning his own shirt as Shoo Ann reached for the button on her jeans.

He forgot what he was doing when she slid the tight jeans off her slender hips.

"Get after it, cowboy. This is not a one-girl hoochy-coochy show," Shoo Ann cackled.

"You bet." Arnold responded. Shoo Ann threw back her head and laughed.

She shed her jeans one leg at a time. For a moment, she stood before him in her panties, and socks. Then she shinnied out of her nylon underwear and laid back on the red blanket.

"Help yourself!"

Arnold wasted no time in stripping off the rest of his clothes and knelt over her in the bed made of hay and blanket. His manhood had reacted instantly the minute she had revealed the flesh beneath her shirt. He was ready to go, big, hard, and long. Shoo Ann noticed and reached down to guide him straight to her body's entry.

Arnold braced himself on his hands and arched into the hot moist fist of her. He pressed deep and Shoo Ann gave a slight gasp of pleasure. Her eyes, always narrow, were almost slits now looking up into his face.

Shoo Ann reached for his buttocks and pressed him to her, rotating her hips against him as if to see if she could engulf him more deeply.

For a few minutes, their breathes mingled as their bodies exalted in the contact. Warmth became heat. A fine coating of sweat covered both of them. Then, Shoo Ann arched her neck back and let a groan leave her lips as her body convulsed in the pleasure of completion. Arnold watched for a second, but any control he could maintain gave way and he pumped fast and hard into her as her hips arched higher to meet his every thrust.

Slowly, Arnold relaxed over Shoo Ann, keeping his weight off her on his arms and elbows but letting his torso and hips touch down on her smooth skin. They laid there. The blanket was wrinkled beneath them but still sheltering their skin from the prickly hay. Arnold lay his head beside Shoo Ann's and slept. His weight, gradually pressing onto her.

Shoo Ann dozed, unconcerned that anyone should come in the barn and see them. Beth had left on a trip while Arnold was gone, not that Beth would have cared about Shoo Ann and Arnold having sex, she would have joined them.

"Beth is gone. Did you know?" Shoo Ann whispered in Arnold's ear. Arnold woke with a start.

"Hmm?"

"Beth is traveling with the Catholic nuns. They located three facilities like the one they want to open for the homeless program. They are visiting the facilities to see how other organizations run their homes and schools. They are looking for good ideas and for errors to avoid."

"She told me on the phone before I left Oklahoma," Arnold's voice was muffled in the blanket.

"She has become a nasty mother bear since the designers presented a building design for the homeless shelter that she did not like and progress on the project has been so slow. It is good she is gone on a trip. She can get her bad temper out of her system, and we can enjoy life."

As she finished, Shoo Ann pushed Arnold off of her and rolled on top of him. As she straddled him, he hardened again and she took charge, setting an even rhythm of sexual in and out.

Arnold's mind went blank. All thoughts of Beth and her temper disappeared as he concentrated on Shoo Ann's lovely face above him and on the sensations her body was imposing on his. When he could take it no longer, he wrapped his arms around her and flipped their positions without losing contact at the groin. His climax was powerful and tipped Shoo Ann over into another of her own.

This time, Arnold fell to his side. Some of the hay tickled his back. He laid Shoo Ann's head on his arm, nestled her against him, pulled the blanket up against the cold, and the two fell into a deep sleep. Neither knew or cared how long they slept, and Sweetheart and Black Shadow watched over them, sleeping on their feet as horses do.

They awoke slowly and dressed, watching each other.

"We are fortunate to have healthy free bodies that can enjoy one another no strings attached," Shoo Ann said stretching her arms over her head in satisfaction.

Arnold grunted.

"I am fortunate that you have such a large and hard—member," Shoo Ann giggled watching Arnold with one eye open and one closed.

Arnold snorted, or maybe it was Black Shadow. No one knew.

Shoo Ann buttoned the last button on her shirt, threw on her coat, let Sweetheart out into the pasture, and headed for the house. Arnold followed more slowly. He had to brush a lot of hay and dust off his suit coat.

Maggie came walking toward him from the house wrapped in a warm blue coat over her blue dress; her hair up in a bun on the back of her neck.

"How are you doing Maggie," Arnold greeted her. "No apron today? Are you making a profit since you became the owner of the restaurant?"

"Yes, I am. I am making more than anyone expected, and I have negotiated with the suppliers a lower price for my foodstuffs and soft drinks. Beginning the first of the month, I will start paying 15% less for all foods and 25% less for soft drinks. Now, I will make more of a profit."

"Excellent," Arnold approved. Have you thought about negotiating with the Catholic Nun organization to provide their supplies when they get that school and home for girls into operation?"

"I have not but will soon now that you mention it. When will Beth and the nuns return?" she asked.

"They left last Sunday and plan to return this Thursday."

"Are you getting lonely?" she asked.

"Sometimes."

"Well I have to return to the restaurant. Come on up for dinner. I close the doors at 9:30 PM."

On Thursday morning, Beth and the nuns returned. Beth dropped the nuns off at their home at 10:30. She arrived at the Beth Ranch at 3:00 pm. She was welcomed by Shoo Ann and Alice with hugs.

"I am exhausted and ready for relaxation and rest, Beth said. She still seemed a little out of sorts, but more relaxed, and not at all excited about the results of the facility tour.

When Arnold asked what she had learned she said abruptly, "to avoid what other people do."

"Maybe you can be more specific later over drinks. I'd like to hear what you are thinking, but first, I think Shoo Ann and Alice need to come to the barn."

Arnold had been monitoring the status of Willy's mare and he was pretty sure she was coming into heat.

"Love is in the air at the barn," Arnold said and winked at Alice.

Shoo Ann and Alice followed him to the barn. Beth decided to come too.

"Why don't you open the gates, Shoo Ann, so Black Shadow and the mare can get together. The stallion needs to tend to his responsibilities," Arnold suggested.

Shoo Ann swung the gates open and Black Shadow was more than ready. His neck was arched as he darted straight to the mare. The mare whinnied and threw only one half-hearted kick in the stallion's direction then settled down and stood perfectly still so Black Shadow could do his work.

Black Shadow rose up over the mare and penetrated her fully. The musky smell of horse semen filled the air and drifted towards the human observers. After retreating, Black Shadow reentered, taking action to ensure against failure, and remained inside the mare for a long time.

Shoo Ann, Alice, and even Beth who was already experienced in ranch life, looked on with curiosity and eagerness.

"This is how new life starts," Alice whispered in awe.

"Shoo Ann, when you get back to the house will you write the date of the mating in the farm logbook and then calculate approximately when the foal will arrive?" Arnold asked.

"Sure Boss."

Later at the ranch house, Arnold got Beth a coffee and poured himself a whiskey. He lifted Beth's feet onto the couch so she could relax and sat down in the armchair next to the couch. The scent of sex lingered in the air. Arnold wondered if it was stuck in his nostrils after watching Black Shadow or if Beth smelled of semen. His eyes narrowed as he looked her over.

"So, what happened on your trip?" Arnold asked meeting her blue eyes that had been so disgruntled when she arrived home. They looked a little happier now that she was home, and her feet were up.

"Everyone needs do better by the girls or we should not enter into this project," she stated.

He waited for her to be more specific.

"Everything the homes offered the girls they sheltered was of low quality, the food, the drinks, the living quarters. It was all poor at every facility."

Arnold asked what the administrative nun thought of the facilities.

"She agrees with me that we cannot duplicate any of the programs we saw administered at any of the three facilities we visited. They were unclean. They were not fit for human occupancy. In fact, we could not understand why the Colorado Health Department had not shut them down. They each housed five times more girls than they can accommodate."

"Are you sorry you went on the tour" Arnold asked.

"I am happy I went. Now I know what not to do." But tears began to run down her cheeks.

"Arnold, it was so sad. These homeless girls have no alternatives. We met three five-year-old girls that I want to adopt right away. Honey, I can't forget them. What can we do?" she cried.

Arnold got up and joined Beth on the couch. He lifted her and sat her on his lap and cradled her. She buried her head in his shoulder while she wept.

"I want to adopt them," she sniffled.

CHAPTER 18

Arnold and Beth ate breakfast early the next morning. He was thinking as he drank his coffee, "She wants to adopt three little girls!"

He began to think they needed even more help than Willy. They needed another hand, one experienced at ranch work and willing to serve as a rover, half time at the Janell Ranch and half time at the Beth Ranch. He reviewed the amount of money they expected the ranch to make. Really, they should wait until they sold some if not all the 75 steers they were grazing. But, he rationalized, he could provide the up-front money for the third hand and let Beth pay him back when the calves were sold and this would prevent him from being tied down all the time. I must avoid getting myself into the position of being responsible for the success or failure of the Beth Ranch. He was building a home in Oklahoma, building a home for himself there.

Arnold looked up at Beth and suggested they hire another hired man.

"I think that is a good idea," she said. Arnold wondered if she was thinking of the three girls she wanted to adopt. That would mean a lot of extra work for her and Shoo Ann and Alice.

"Will you write the ad and I'll post it at the restaurant?" Beth asked agreeably.

Within two days three applicants responded. Beth and he conducted the interviews. Only two had the necessary qualifications they needed. Beth decided on one that seemed to both of them to be the best choice. The man, Larry Harper, also seemed to need the work so they hoped he would work hard and stay on.

Larry Harper was 26 years old and he lived with his parents about six miles north of Alamosa. His hair was jet black and his beard was shaved but got heavy toward the end of the day. He was a little over 6 feet tall and strong. He drove a late model Ford F-150 pick-up and needed to make large payments. He agreed to start on Monday.

By the end of the first week, Arnold and Willy were happy with Larry. He displayed an enthusiasm that was impressive. He was knowledgeable about ranch work and strong enough to get it done.

Arnold was thinking of returning to Oklahoma to check on his house construction since everything was going so well at the Beth Ranch and the Janell Ranch.

As he was riding Black Shadow back to the Beth Ranch from the leased land at the Janell Ranch one afternoon, he encountered Janell on the side of the road trying to get her pick-up to start.

"Damned Jalopy," she hollered into his ear when he joined her where she was leaning over the engine red faced. He just grinned and stuck his finger in his ear. Then he helped her make two adjustments in the carburetor and it fired perfectly. Janell got back in the cab of her "damned jalopy" and her dress rode up her thighs, wrapped halfway to her waist. Arnold could not help staring. He was pretty sure his mouth dropped open too.

Janell caught him looking and instead of covering up encouraged him by adjusting her dress upward until he could see all the way up her strong white legs to her panties.

All he could think to say was, "Beautiful. Beautiful," and then, "I must get out of here." He mounted Black Shadow as if a swarm of bumblebees were after him.

Janell threw back her head and laughed. She said, "It will keep, so hurry back when you have more time."

When Arnold walked into the ranch house later that evening, Beth said, "I have something important to say." He stood in the living room hanging up his hat and coat while she continued, her hands setting on her slim hips while she talked and paced around the room. Arnold's eyes followed her.

"We should not act on emotion concerning the girls in the Catholic home for homeless girls. We must be smart about this because their future is uncertain, and it would not be right to make a mistake. I would love to raise children since I can't have any of my own. But what if I am terrible at it?"

Hearing this last part, Arnold jumped into the one-sided conversation, "In my opinion, we should go to Oklahoma for Christmas, review my business matters and talk this over. Then we can decide what our next step should be."

Beth stopped pacing and looked at him her head tilted as if she had a question.

Arnold continued before she could say anything to this proposition. "As to the five-year-old girls, we cannot just forget them, not even one of them." Arnold heard his own voice rise as emotion and passion for helping the vulnerable girls filled him. "You were quite convinced they needed help when you told me about them the other day. You cried!"

Beth looked at him in wonder.

"We can help them Beth. I know we can."

Even Arnold wondered where his new conviction was coming from. Maybe, the Lord had been silently working on him.

Arnold called the airlines and scheduled a flight for two to depart the next day for Oklahoma City. The flight included reservations for a rental car and a motel in El Reno.

"What do you need to see in Oklahoma that would make a difference in our decision regarding the five-year-old girls?" asked Beth as they drove to the airport the next morning.

"I don't need to see anything, but we need time, time to think this through," Arnold said. "I know what I am prepared to do, but I'm not sure what you are prepared to do. So, we need some time together."

Then he said, "we need to talk about the long-term commitment involved in caring for the five-year-old girls who might not be very stable given all they have been through."

"Explain. Be specific," Beth said.

"We know nothing about these girls. We do not know about their physical or mental capabilities or lack thereof, and we are perhaps not prepared to care for children who have unbelievably complex health conditions." Arnold explained.

"We could grow to love these girls. Hopefully, we do. I had a friend who adopted a child and cared for him deeply. Ultimately, the boy committed suicide at 15. My friend lost his mind for a while. It caused him grief he had never known before or since. He often felt guilty and extremely sad because of this loss and because he knew the boy had problems, but he blamed himself for his suicide and his own limitations in caring for him."

Arnold continued "I realize we must do all they can for the unfortunate ones we encounter in our lives, but we must be aware of reality that the task is sometimes overwhelming. We need to be rational about it, use common sense, and avoid taking on something we do not have the knowledge or skill to deal with. We think we are smart people but there are situations about which we know nothing."

Beth began to cry. "I couldn't imagine living with any of these girls dying so young. Give me time," she muttered.

By then, they had arrived at the Pueblo Airport. They held onto each other and cried for a long time before composing themselves enough to enter the terminal.

The flight to Oklahoma City was uneventful. In the airport there, they were advised to wait in the airport as an unusually strong storm was passing nearby. They sat and waited with dozens of other people for the storm to pass. Arnold was anxious to pick up their rental car and continue to El Reno and Calumet. Thunder and lightning accompanied the snow and caused him to wonder if they needed to locate a storm shelter.

Soon the heavier snow passed, and they were on their way to the interstate. All was quiet. Very few cars were on the road. Arriving at their motel, in El Reno, they ordered Chinese food and had it delivered to their room. While they ate, they discussed the possibility of adopting the five-year-old girls.

Beth asked if it was possible to investigate their health, their well-being, and their level and capability to learn. Arnold thought it was possible. He was pretty sure there would be a file on each girl that they could see before deciding to adopt.

As Arnold and Beth ate eggs and toast and drank coffee the next morning, Arnold announced out of the blue, "I think, we need to return to Oklahoma City and visit a jewelry store before we head to Calumet."

Beth dropped her fork into her egg yolk. "What? Am I understanding you right or am I dreaming, jewelry store?"

"No. You are not dreaming. This is the real deal. We need to initiate a more complete future for the two of us, don't you think? We can't raise children without marrying. And it is Christmas Eve! What would be a better gift than a ring?"

Beth laughed happily and agreed it would be a nice day to look at rings.

Instead of going all the way back to Oklahoma City, they stopped at a jewelry store in the town of Yukon. Within 10 minutes, Beth had picked out the ring she wanted. Arnold bought it. Tucking the little package in his pocket, he said, "to be given at a later date."

Beth frowned like a mother bear but could not dissuade him from waiting. He had other plans and was determined to make it work, his way.

Beth pouted a little but got over it quickly as they drove onto the construction site where his new house was being built. Inside, they found that they were alone for it was still early, and the construction workers were not yet at work. Once inside, he spun around and grinned at Beth, "Will you accept the ring now?"

Beth opened her mouth and let out a screech. "Yes. Yes," she said when she got her normal voice back.

It was a joy for him to experience her happiness. They crawled all over the house and looked in every corner.

"This will be ours," Arnold said.

"When shall we get married?" Beth asked. "I mean, can we set the date?"

"Sweetheart. I can't yet, one giant leap for this boy at a time."

"Okay," she agreed without further argument.

They drove to the office of D, D, and C and the secretary informed them that Arnold's investment balance was $108 million. She told him he needed to discuss further investments with the partners."

Beth leaned over and whispered to the secretary, "how much of this is Arnold's?"

"Sweetheart, all of it," the secretary responded with a chuckle.

Upon returning to their rental car, Beth said, "I simply cannot believe this. It is unbelievable."

Arnold simply said, "Now is when we must remember to use sound judgment and not let our emotions get us in trouble."

They grinned at each other and hugged. They looked over the land Arnold had recently purchased and stopped by the bank to say hello to

Robert. Arnold was grateful that Charlene did not happen to be there even though she and Beth had met before.

They enjoyed the afternoon and dinner but began to worry how things were going on the Beth Ranch with the addition of 150 cows and leased ranch land. Arnold changed their return tickets for the next morning and they went to bed early practicing for their marriage in the squeaky motel bed.

Upon their arrival to the Beth Ranch, they were somewhat embarrassed to find that their concern was unjustified because everything had been handled properly and was running smoothly. Shoo Ann and Alice were preparing a Christmas dinner. Beth joined in the work.

Arnold was delighted because he wanted to ride out on Black Shadow to his favorite location among the trees and see the frozen little brook. He was sitting beside the stream on Black Shadow when a mountain lion made its appearance. Black Shadow started to dance. It only took three shots from his 30-06 and the lion took off. Arnold was happy to see that Black Shadow did not flinch at the gun shots taken from his back. The stallion settled down to pawing at the snow for the remnants of grass.

Arnold enjoyed a long ride around the ranch and then headed back to the ranch house for Christmas dinner. Beth rode up on Autumn Time and joined him on the ride back. She wanted to discuss the five-year-old girls again and hear his plan to learn more about them.

"We will need to hire an investigator to find out everything we want to know discreetly to protect the girls from disappointment if we decide we cannot adopt them," he explained. "And we will need to hire a lawyer who is capable of handling multiple adoptions.

"I really did not know it would be so complicated," Beth said

"The sticky situation I went through with my divorce taught me the value of a good lawyer," he assured Beth. "We can start by talking to a lawyer that is experienced in dealing with adoptions and let him hire the investigator. We can then consult him about everything that comes up."

"That sounds like a good idea," Beth said.

To change the subject, he asked Beth if her ring fit her finger.

Beth brought Autumn Time alongside Black Shadow and grabbed Arnold by the collar of his coat. She drew his face to hers across the space between the horses.

"You bet it does. You are not going to take it back," she laughed.

He lunged for her hand. He took off her glove and kissed her fingers. With his teeth he pulled on the diamond and twisted the ring. His tongue played between her fingers and Beth squealed.

"That tickles," she yelled.

She took off on Autumn Time at full speed and Black Shadow soon caught up. By the time they reached the barn, the horses were snorting large plumes of mist. They jumped off their horses and Arnold wrapped Beth in his arms.

She nuzzled his neck and then in revenge tickled his ribs. They wrestled playfully until clothes started coming off and the situation got highly and happily serious.

As she stripped him, Beth explored every inch of Arnold's body with her hands and lips as if he were a precious artifact. She left no stone unturned. Arnold snagged a blanket and laid it on the stacked hay bales. He tried to lay back passively and enjoy the sensations she created, but soon he was peeling off her clothes and had her tipped her over returning the favor. His lips traveled over her marvelous breasts, suckled her tight nipples, and cut wet trails down her belly to trace the fading scars down to her bushy patch of pubic hair. She let out a gasp as he moved lower and with hands and lips explored the lips of her vulva and the moist cavern of her vagina. Her response was electric, and she shuddered with delight as she came before he entered her.

Arnold was learning where sensations were strongest on her newly made sexual anatomy. He liked having her naked under his hands. He liked learning what touches aroused her and what touches did nothing.

Her body worked a bit differently than the bodies of other women because it had been recreated from a male foundation.

He carefully slid his engorged penis into her vagina and moved gently at first always mindful of his size and the possibility of damaging her. Soon he forgot his care and set a rhythm that had them both breathing in gasps. Beth let out a cry as she came a second time with Arnold's penis inside her and he groaned as his body felt her tremors and followed her lead into oblivion and satisfaction.

They lay in a lazy heap of limbs in the grey light of the barn and pulled their winter coats over their bare skin. They listened to the wind in the rafters and to the munching of their contented mounts. Black Shadow was eating oats from the manger. Autumn Time was waiting her turn, filling time eating great mouthfuls of hay. Every now and then the big stallion shifted his feet and swished his tail.

"Merry Christmas Beth."

"Merry Christmas Arnold."

"I expect many more gifts just like that last one," Arnold murmured.

"Aye," Beth agreed in a whisper. "That will not be a problem."

CHAPTER 19

Arnold contacted David Baker, the banker in Alamosa, for a referral to a local lawyer capable of helping them deal with adoption. A week had gone by before Baker returned his call, and two more weeks went by before the lawyer returned his call. The lawyer's name was Alan Fontaine. He apologized for his delay in getting back to Arnold and blamed the holidays. As they introduced themselves, Arnold learned that Fontaine had 15 years of experience in family law and adoption. Their conversation was general until Arnold informed Fontaine that he wanted to retain him. Following this clarification, they got down to business. Fontaine informed Arnold of the process they would need to follow, the type of investigator he would need to hire, and the cost associated with the entire procedure.

"It is not cheap," Alan said, "and could cost more depending on the amount of time it took to establish the facts."

"I'd like you to proceed if you will," Arnold stated.

"My retainer is $3,000.00."

"That is not a problem. It will be in the form of a cashiers' check drawn on the First National Bank of Calumet, Oklahoma. Why don't we meet tomorrow in Alamosa at your office and Beth Howser will be with me?'

"Does 10:00 AM work for you?"

Both Beth and Arnold thought Alan was very professional. He seemed to really know his business. The meeting was informative, but preliminary and raised more questions in their minds than it answered. Beth and Arnold left the Fontaine's office wanting time to pass quickly so they could get the answers they wanted. Waiting was hard. They wanted to make a decision one way or the other, but without information, they would be flying blindly while changing the lives of some young girls, not to mention their own. They tried to be patient.

It was three weeks before they received a call from Alan Fontaine. They were putting out hay for the cows at the time of the call but dropped their ranch work and drove over to meet with him at his office. Beth and Arnold listened intently only to learn that the process of getting the kind of background and health information on the girls was going to be a slow one.

"I'm sorry to have so little information yet," apologized Fontaine when he realized they had expected more from him. "I just wanted to tell you about the investigator I have found and explain the ethical hurdles."

"I should have expected that," admitted Arnold. "I don't know why we thought you would have the information already."

Beth was silent as they walked back to the truck and most of the way back to the Beth Ranch.

Another several weeks went by and Fontaine again called them in for a meeting. This time, they learned the names and ages and health conditions of each of the 5-year-old girls. Alan told them there were eight of them in the first group they asked to be evaluated.

"The investigator said that each of the girls has a sister that is two years older, and it would be necessary to take all 10 girls or none because they cannot be split up or otherwise separated."

Beth and Arnold went home to consider their strategy.

"Ten girls are too much for them to handle. Don't you think?" Beth asked.

"Definitely," Arnold agreed.

"What will happen to the $3,000 retainer if we cancel?"

"The money is gone," Arnold stated.

Beth started to cry quietly.

"Maybe there is an option we can consider. Instead of adoption, maybe we can request the ten girls be transferred to the facility in Alamosa where you and I and the nuns can look after them closely?" suggested Arnold.

Beth stopped crying, listened to Arnold's suggestion, and began to smile."

The smile got broader the more she thought through the idea. "This idea is better than adoption and me trying to care for that many children. I am confident this will work. At least the chances of it being approved are greater than the chances of you and I adopting 10 girls."

When they had reached the Beth Ranch, Beth got out of the car and asked, "Shall we proceed as though this is now our plan?"

"Yes." Arnold said without hesitating.

Beth called Sister Mary Frances. She told the nun what they had been trying to do by adopting the 5-year-old girls and told her what they had found out about the 7-year-old sisters.

"I know the local home will be full, with no room left, but what if we expand the facility so it can hold 20 girls?"

Sister Mary Frances was agreeable, and she agreed to help Beth push for an expansion for this purpose.

The very next day Beth was notified of an urgent meeting of the organizers of the Catholic Nunn facility for homeless girls.

Alan Fontaine called and told them that nothing had come up on the girls that would prevent them for being adopted or transferred to the new facility.

During the meeting, the expansion plans were approved, and Arnold asked Alan Fontaine to begin paperwork for the transfer the 10 girls to the new facility in Alamosa. Each facility of the facilities currently housing the girls received the news with open arms because they were so overcrowded.

With this decided and while they were still sitting in the meeting, Arnold suggested that Beth begin planning her strategy to become an influential member of the Administrative Board.

How much do you think you will have to donate to ensure you get on the board?" he asked.

Beth thought it over for a moment. She looked in her purse and retrieved the piece of paper on which she had written the balance of Arnold's Oklahoma investments. She held it out so Arnold could see it.

He looked at the paper then over to the ornery expression on her face.

"Well. Not that much," she said laughing. Arnold broke into laugher too.

Beth talked with the Sister Mary Frances and asked if she could do anything to pave the way for the girls' transfer. Everyone agreed there was a lot of work that needed to be done to prepare for the girls once the building was complete. Together they made a list of projects that needed completion. Beth promised the nun that she would take responsibility for completing each of the items and would organize volunteers to assist.

Beth and Arnold returned to the ranch feeling relieved and triumphant. They picked up on their chores where they had left off several days earlier. Fortunately, Willy and Larry were making a great team and almost without discussion assisted each other with all the jobs that took more than one person. Periodically, Shoo Ann pitched in and helped.

Three months went by without anyone really noticing. It was now spring. Beth was working the transfer issues for the girls and overseeing construction crews working on the building that would house the home for homeless girls. Willy and Larry and Shoo Ann were monitoring newborn calves.

One afternoon, Shoo Ann told Beth that she wanted to show her some of the things on the ranch she thought important. Beth and Shoo Ann saddled their horses and rode east toward the area fenced off for the goats. Sometimes the llamas joined the goats because they could jump the electric fence without difficulty whenever they wanted to.

When Shoo Ann and Beth arrived at the goats' pasture, they noticed almost twice as many goats as Arnold had purchased. The goats had obviously multiplied more quickly than he expected. The weeds and underbrush were gone, which was Arnold's goal in getting the goats in the first place.

At the southeastern-most section of the goat area, larger trees dominated and there was very little underbrush.

"It is time to rest the horses," Shoo Ann said to Beth.

"At home in Indonesia, I'd spread the blankets out here for our relaxation, but it is not yet warm enough for that here. We would freeze our bums off," Shoo Ann said as the two dismounted.

Beth soon realized how long it had been since she and Shoo Ann had been alone.

"I think everything on the ranch looks great. It looks to me like you have taken care of everything Shoo Ann. Let's head back to the house while everyone else is out working for a little break where it is warmer."

Riding back to the ranch house, they talked about ranch work and Shoo Ann reminded her that Willy and his family could use several of the young goats because they liked to eat goat meat.

"I think we should only keep 20 goats," Shoo Ann said.

"Willy get ready for some goats," Beth said facetiously.

"The goats keep the lions away from the cows with calves. I saw a lion kill at least 4 goats for food. Arnold did not get the goats for that purpose, but it has turned out to be an added benefit.

The women approached the barn and dismounted. They rubbed down their mounts, drying them and settling them in their stalls with buckets of oats and nearby water.

Beth caught Shoo Ann by her elbow and ushered her into the ranch house. All was quiet. Everyone was out working at some task on the ranch or at the restaurant. She continued to pull Shoo Ann into the bedroom, not the one she shared with Arnold, but the smaller one with the narrow bed where Shoo Ann slept.

The two women stood nose to nose when the door shut. The smiled into each other's eyes. Slowly they kissed. They removed their clothes and laid down together on the single bed, face to face still smiling at each other. Beth stroked Shoo Ann's breasts very gently. They moved closer and closer until Beth's hand was caught between their bodies. She lowered it to Shoo Ann's sex and gently prodded as Shoo Anne ran her long thin fingers over Beth buttock.

"Mmmm," Shoo Ann sighed.

Beth prodded more vigorously with her strong middle finger.

"Mmmm," Shoo Ann groaned and tightened her grip on Beth's butt cheeks. Her face was pressed into Beth's full right breast.

Beth caressed Shoo Ann's shoulder with her tongue and was rewarded by the flicker of Shoo Ann's tongue against her nipple. Shoo Ann suckled.

Beth ran her finger quickly around the moist edges of Shoo Ann's sex, again and again. She dipped her finger into Shoo Ann's center.

"Mmmm," Shoo Ann cried out against Beth's breast, opening her lips to get more air into her lungs.

Entwined the two women continued to touch and sip at each other. Shoo Ann pulled Beth's thighs up on either side of her own body so she could reach Beth's vagina between her parted legs and probing deeply found the sensitive flesh at the very depths that responded abruptly to the gentle touch.

Both women gripped hard and cried out as they climaxed wrapped together so it was hard to tell where one woman ended, and one began. Only their heads gave them away, one black, one brown.

They stretched, untangled, and laid alongside each other until they drifted off to sleep.

When they woke, the house was still quiet. They looked in each other's eyes. They had been friends for several years now. They knew each other. They trusted each other. They smiled, and both said and heard the other say, "Mmmm."

Beth swung her legs over the edge of the bed and Shoo Ann followed. They dressed without talking all the way to putting their coats back on. They hugged and opened the bedroom door into the warm living room.

"I'm getting hungry," Shoo Ann said.

They opened the outside door to the house and headed to the barn where Willy, Larry, and Arnold were just putting their horses into their stalls with oats and water.

"Let's go to the restaurant tonight," Beth suggested to everyone.

"I'm hungry," said Willy.

"I'm hungry," said Larry.

"I'm hungry," said Arnold the last to leave behind his horse.

"I'll have a guest, said Larry. "She helped me repair the fence this morning."

Arnold and Beth looked at Shoo Ann.

"Not me," she said with her hands in the air.

"No not Shoo Ann. It is a surprise," confirmed Larry as he climbed into the truck with Willy while the others got into Arnold's truck.

They all sat a few minutes warming up the vehicles before heading to Maggie's restaurant.

"When they got to the restaurant, Larry hugged a tall woman with wild beige hair. Her hair curled in all directions, seeming to prefer up to all the rest. Arnold and Beth and Shoo Ann stared bemused by the woman's hair.

"This is Larry's wife, Geraldine," laughed Willy. "She sometimes accompanies Larry to work when the kids are in school."

"Nice to meet you," came out of three mouths all at once. It was nice to get acquainted with Geraldine. The number at their favorite table kept increasing.

That made Maggie smile as she brought out the menus.

CHAPTER 20

B eth woke Arnold early the next morning. She wanted to talk.
"Come on Arnold, wake up. I'll make you some coffee."

Arnold looked at her through one eye. The other refused to open and admit he was awake.

"Arnold the homeless girls are arriving sooner than planned. I'm not sure the facility will be ready for them. What should I do?" Beth whispered in his ear.

Arnold rolled himself out of bed and pulled his clothes on while Beth went out to the kitchen to make coffee. It was so early Shoo Ann was not up yet. She usually made the morning coffee.

At the kitchen table, nursing a hot cup of coffee, Arnold tried to wake up so he would be able to advise Beth.

The homes where the children lived wanted to relocate the children now.

"I think you need to call an emergency meeting of the board that will be governing the home. You need to know exactly how far along the building is and how many of the staff has been hired. Then review alternatives and prioritize. You may have to refuse to take the girls at this time," Arnold warned.

As soon as the clock hit 8:00 AM, Beth called each member of the board and asked them to schedule an emergency meeting as soon as possible.

"I really want the construction expedited so that the building and staff are ready for the day of relocation," said Beth.

"Can you make that decision without the approval of the board?" Arnold asked.

"I don't want to miss the transfer date and lose the support of the people supporting the program."

"You need to stand firm at the meeting. Push for the option you want to be implemented and be firm in your approach. I mean do not back down," advised Arnold

Beth smiled, "This will be difficult for me."

"But you can do it if you think it is the right thing to do," Arnold encouraged her. "Beth let's go get the horses and ride over to the restaurant for breakfast," Arnold suggested.

It did not take long for them both to have their mounts ready to go. As they headed toward the restaurant, the horses moved at a brisk walk, throwing their heads around friskily every now and then. The fresh morning air cleared their heads. Arnold could tell that Beth was getting stronger and had completely recovered from her surgery.

He was certain that Beth could develop into a leader. The board certainly needed one. He observed at the last meeting that they were a passive bunch except for Sister Mary Francis and Beth.

After they had tied their horses to the hitching post that Maggie still had in front of the restaurant for her riding customers, they entered the dining room, found a table and ordered coffee, eggs over easy with bacon and toast.

While they waited for their food to arrive, Arnold repeated that he thought Beth should prepare a presentation of the options and timelines and present it at the start of the meeting.

"Maybe someone else should make the presentation," Beth suggested.

"Why don't you want to do it?" Arnold asked.

"Because, I have never made a presentation before."

"So, this may be the first, but it should not be the last," Arnold replied.

"You are persistent," Beth said.

"But not as persistent as I am going to be when they get home, to bed."

Beth gave him a look that told him she understood perfectly where he was going.

A new waitress delivered their food to them. After eating a couple of mouthfuls, Beth said, "I'll do it. As soon as we get home, I'll call the banker and tell him I have an important item for the agenda and would like to present it first."

"That's the spirit."

Arnold knew Beth was on her way to achieving her goal with the homeless shelter for girls.

When Beth and Arnold rode back into the ranch yard, they found Willy packing supplies in his truck. Shoo Ann had already departed on Sweetheart for the goat pasture. She and Willy were going to identify about 10 of the fattest young goats for Willy to take home with him. According to Willy, his wife was thrilled at the prospect of receiving new goats and the children were also excited.

Alice was just leaving the house, heading for the barn.

"Would you look at how I saddle my pony?" she called out to Arnold. "I want to make sure I'm doing everything right."

Arnold watched Alice saddle her pony and made no suggestions except to ensure the blanket was smooth and straight under the saddle. He got down from Black Shadow and made a slight adjustment to demonstrate the importance of this detail for the comfort of the horse.

"You have learned a lot since this all began," Arnold complemented her as he swung back into the saddle.

"Yes. I have," Alice responded happily. "I'm going to help Shoo Ann and Willy round up 10 goats."

Since he was already mounted on Black Shadow, Arnold decided to ride along with Alice and oversee the goat operation.

"You haven't named that horse yet," Arnold pointed out to Alice.

"I know. It takes a lot of thought," Alice responded.

Black Shadow and Alice's pony glided across the prairie. Arnold went into a kind of trance, a dreamland, where he did not notice anything except the cool breeze hitting him in the face and the soothing rhythm of a lope. He even failed to notice that Alice had ridden on to the goat pasture without him.

Black Shadow slowed and stopped at Arnold's favorite place out of habit or Arnold would have missed it. He dismounted, retrieved his thermos bottle for another cup of coffee and the blanket to sit on from his saddle bags.

He loved ranching, Arnold thought. What is in store for me when I quit working on the ranch and move back to Oklahoma?

This thought had already occurred to him on the way to the restaurant and it had depressed him then and still did now. He asked himself, "Why are you thinking of quitting work on the ranch?"

You have done well, Arnold thought to himself, why think negatively about any of it? For a man who started out with no money a year or so ago, you have landed in the best situation anyone could ever have, great people to be around, the best of food and rest facilities, reliable people to help work the ranch and the best of females ever. Return to your optimistic self and let it be.

Resting on his elbows, Arnold observed Willy drive by with a pick-up loaded with goats. Soon after, Shoo Ann rode up on Sweetheart.

"Can I offer you a cup of coffee?"

"No. Is that all you have to offer this morning."

Her lopsided beautiful smile told him exactly what she meant, and he quirked his eyebrows and patted the blanket next to him.

"That is better," Shoo Ann grinned as she jumped down from Sweetheart and looped the reins around the same branch Black Shadow was tied to. Arnold stood up and he and Shoo Ann began stripping. They laughed at each other and began to race. Buttons came undone. Jeans were unzipped. Boots were kicked off. Arnold won because he had on less clothes. He grabbed Shoo Ann around the waist as she tried to run away from him still in her bra and socks.

She giggled as he raised her feet off the ground so she could not get traction enough to run. He swung her up into his arms and carried her to the blanket. He sat down with her in his lap and massaged his free hand between her legs, spreading her. She tilted her head back on his shoulder, her eyes closed to mere slits. He leaned down and sealed her lips with his own and his big hand stroked her. His big finger bent and penetrated her warmth.

"Ack," Shoo Ann cried out freeing her lips from his.

He recaptured her lips and withdrawing his finger, he circled her clitoris until he felt it bead in arousal.

Shoo Ann moaned.

"Not the finger," she gasped, freeing her wet lips again. "I want something bigger inside me."

Arnold chuckled and lifted her bodily into the air and turned her to face him. She straddled his hips and pressed down hard over his waiting penis. He pressed her to him and she wrapped her arms around his neck. He rolled her beneath him and they quickly climaxed. Shoo Ann's back was on the rug now and Arnold lay atop her for a moment before he rolled to the side so she could breathe.

"Ah God! That felt good," Shoo Ann sighed.

"Yep it did," agreed Arnold breathing quickly as he lay on his back beside her, the breeze cooling his naked flesh.

They heard the horses shift around and opened their eyes to see Alice eyeing them from atop her pony.

They froze.

"So, you are riding the blanket without the hay bale," she said saucily. "Nice." They heard a shrill wolf whistle then only laughing as she rode away.

As Arnold watched Shoo Ann dress, he thought to himself, "Arnold, this is proof that you are a lucky-lucky man. Now, think more positive thoughts. Acknowledge reality and enjoy the good times.

Shoo Ann rode off, leaving Arnold to snooze naked on his blanket beside the stream for a bit longer.

When Arnold returned to the house, the phone rang. It was D, D, and C informing him the transfer of $3 million had occurred and the bank of Alamosa had acknowledged receipt. He thanked the accounting firm and hung up. He called the Alamosa bank to confirm and requested they inform Beth.

Five minutes passed before Beth called him on one of the phones at the bank. She was thrilled.

"Will news of the transfer help your confidence in dealing with the Board?" Arnold asked.

"Yes. Oh yes. I feel on top of the world. Meet me at Maggie's for a quick lunch." She hung up.

Arnold mounted Black Shadow once again for a ride to the restaurant.

When he sat down at their favorite table at Maggie's, Beth informed him that David Baker, the banker in Alamosa, had also told her the emergency meeting was scheduled for the next day at 10:00 AM.

"I am first on the agenda. I can present my suggestions immediately following his opening remarks about why the emergency meeting was called."

Beth looked happier than he had seen her in a long time.

"This is territory you will find yourself in again and again every time there is an important event dealing with the homeless shelter. Get accustomed to it. Do not let it trouble you at all. Think through the problem, use sound judgment, and take the initiative," Arnold advised.

Arnold reached his arm out and hugged Beth.

Beth turned her smiling face to his. "Are you going to attend the meeting?"

"No. They do not need me when they have you. I plan to be working on the ranch. I need to check on the llamas. Larry called me asking about how much work we wanted to invest in repairing fences at the Janell Ranch. I am meeting him in an hour."

Beth and Arnold went their separate ways after lunch, Beth heading back to Beth Ranch while Arnold headed over to the Janell ranch to meet Larry.

After looking at the fences in question, Arnold asked Larry, "What would you do with them if they were yours?"

"If these fences were mine, I would replace the posts and the wire and stretch the wire tight. If required, I would add cross posts to ensure the wire stays tight."

"In response to your original question and others in a similar situation, repair it your way because the way you suggest is the correct way to repair a fence," Arnold answered.

"Good deal. I'll pick up the supplies and have them send you the bill to be paid."

"Have them make the bill out to Beth Houser. She owns the lease."

Arnold shook hands with Larry and said, "I like the way you think."

CHAPTER 21

The next day, Arnold stopped by the restaurant for an afternoon cup of coffee. He hung his hat up at the door and dropped his gloves into the chair next to him. Maggie brought him a cup of coffee unasked and informed him she had heard from the governing board for the girl's home following their emergency meeting. They are going to expedite completion of the building."

"Beth came in earlier, after the meeting. She was thrilled. The construction company committed to the completion date and the transfers for the twenty girls were going as planned. The girls will be relocated within two weeks."

Arnold grinned as he sipped his coffee. Maggie sat down across from him at the table since the restaurant was empty this time of day. Seeing her boss sitting down, a young waitress brought Maggie a cup of coffee.

"Thanks, Dear," Maggie said and settled in to finish her story.

"I agreed to cater three meals a day for the twenty girls for two weeks. Then, I bid on the contract to provide workers to cook and clean on site. I won that contract!" Maggie laughed.

"Are you going to make money off this transaction?" Arnold asked tentatively, not sure how far he should stick his nose into her business.

"I listened carefully to Beth before I submitted the bid. I understood what they wanted. I will make more money than I have ever made before," she replied. "I need to go to Pueblo soon to order a large amount of supplies, and I would like you to help me. It should not take more than one half day travel over, spend one night and travel back the next day."

"I'll go with you. Just let me know one day advance, and I will be ready."

Arnold and Maggie chatted over coffee before they decided they had both better get back to work. Arnold enjoyed his coffee and the conversation.

On his way back to the Beth Ranch, Arnold began to think again. His thoughts confused him, so he stopped at the barn, sat on a bale of hay, and thought.

He began to think of the day he left Oklahoma, heading west on Highway 66. He recalled he was depressed and confused at the time and did not want to decide where he was going. He was just going. He took little money with him. He did not think he needed much. He wanted experiences. He did not listen to any music or news as he drove. He stopped when he wanted to and drove when he wanted to, all the while avoiding any responsibilities that might be assigned to him. He wanted to be a free man, no attachments, no commitments, no responsibilities.

As he looked back on those thoughts, he felt drowsy again. "All this sex and deep thinking is making me need more naps," he thought before he fell asleep. He woke a short time later when something nuzzled against his shoulder and head. He stirred slowly but did not open his eyes. He experienced a tickle around one ear and along the side of his face. At first, he thought it might be Shoo Ann or Beth or Alice. He smiled. Then, thinking it might be a mouse, he sat up fast. He found he was being studied by the cat that had established residence in the barn. Black Shadow was standing patiently nearby.

He soon discovered the real reason his nap was disturbed. Four small kittens were trying to follow their mother and walked onto him as they did. When he saw the kittens, he frowned. Two of them had fallen into his lap when he sat up. The other two had fallen the other way and were righting themselves in the hay behind him. He did not want a large number of cats in the barn. Then he remembered how many women occupied the ranch house. There were just enough kittens for the women in the house to each own one. From experience he knew that women and kittens soon became inseparable.

Around the supper table that evening, Arnold disclosed the presence of a mother cat and four kittens in the barn. He proposed that he donate them all to the Larry and Willy families, that being two kittens each and one gets a mother cat for being kind and accepting the kittens."

Beth, Alice, and Shoo Ann got quiet and then stared at him in horror as if he had pulled a snake out of his pocket at the dinner table.

"No, no, no," cried Beth.

"One is mine," shouted Alice.

"And — one is mine," stated Shoo Ann.

They all left the table and headed for the barn. Arnold sat alone at the table for a moment studying the food that would soon be cold. He shrugged and followed to observe. The mother cat looked worried as her kittens were being picked up and talked to as if they were humans.

Beth began talking. It seemed to Arnold that she couldn't decide whether to talk about kittens or homeless girls, or Maggie. She paced around the barn and wove the subjects together in a confusing burst of nervous chatter.

"I have news for you, Arnold."

"The kittens should stay in the house instead of the barn. Maggie needs you to take her to Pueblo to purchase supplies for a contract she is going to accept at the facility for the homeless girls. The girls will be transferred here in two weeks. Some could arrive in seven days and will need lodging, food and water and other care. Where will they sleep? Someone needs to help Maggie hire someone to help her."

When Beth finally took a needed breath, Arnold raised his hands over his head and said, "Stop! We must slow down."

Beth grabbed him and kissed him.

"I'm just so happy with it all," she shouted.

"Sweetheart, I believe you," Arnold said and hugged Beth.

He then said to the assembled women, "Please let us go back into the house and finish dinner. Then you can tell me whatever it is you have on your mind."

In the house, he poured himself a scotch to go with the last of his cold dinner and sat back and listened.

Beth talked fast and recapped all that Maggie had told him earlier, adding "The Alamosa Educational and Advancement Home for Homeless Ladies is going to do things correctly. That is the official name of our effort. We will develop a theme and a code of conduct for the staff and for the young ladies in our care. We will have the theme and code ready when the Ladies arrive. Maggie is going to talk with you about the contract, purchase of supplies, and ways to establish a business separate from the restaurant and motel. She wants to operate the catering and cooking for the Home for Homeless Ladies as a separate business entity. She wants to talk with you about all of this. When she bid the contract, she asked me how much she should bid. I told her to bid enough to make at least 20% profit, and if she chooses to take a lower profit it later, she can refund some of the money she makes."

Waving her hands, she said, "Arnold, I suggest we go over to the restaurant tonight for coffee and pie. We can plan some of this with Maggie. And remember, I have a meeting at 8:00 PM tonight with the banker, the administration person for the home, and with four nuns to prepare the job description of each employee to be hired.

Beth continued while Arnold sipped his scotch and did not interrupt.

"You and Maggie will need to finish your discussions after she gets off work at the restaurant. I should be home by 10:00 PM or a bit later."

Arnold asked Beth if she would be able to slow down enough to eat dinner. She smiled and said, "Let's skip it and go for coffee and pie right now. All this is cold anyway." Alice and Shoo Ann stayed to finish eating and to do the dishes.

Beth ate a piece of pie and took off for Alamosa for her meeting with the banker and other facility officials. Maggie and Arnold decided to go to pueblo the next day for supplies.

As far as extra help was concerned, Maggie said she had already hired a local lady, Maxine, to work for her. She called Maxine out of the office and introduced her to Arnold.

He stood and extended his hand to shake hers. The woman nodded but did not reach her hand out to accept his. Arnold studied her. The woman was Maggie's age but plump and her hair might have been dyed black for it showed not a hint of grey.

"I know you," Maxine said. "You purchased a pickup from the Chevrolet dealer. I prepared the paperwork for that sale."

Arnold acknowledged that he had bought a pickup almost a year ago.

"I also remembered you paid cash and ordered all the amenities. That cost a lot of money. I helped prepare the paperwork for many sales, but that was the only one we sold for cash."

"Maxine, I also remember you because you did not want to shake hands with me when I bought the pickup and today you also refused. This is okay, but when you do things differently from other people it causes a person like me to wonder why. So why don't you shake hands?"

Maxine smiled. "I'm sorry. I am shy and seldom shake hands with men."

"I see," Arnold replied. "I am pleased to meet you and will probably see more of you now that you are working for Maggie."

"I hope so," said Maxine and turned to return the restaurant's office.

Arnold turned back to Maggie. "Beth tells me that you might have questions for me about the contract and how to set up a separate business for that line or work in the future.

Maggie looked towards the office and said, "We should go to my suite in the motel where we can discuss this in private."

Arnold had almost forgotten that she had a suite in the motel that adjoined the restaurant. She was the owner of both establishments and when he had first arrived in Alamosa he had rented a room from her.

Maggie was right. Her suite was nice and comfortable and private. Maggie poured coffee and they studied the menu she had prepared and the list of food stuffs, equipment, and supplied she planned to buy tomorrow.

"I'm going to negotiate a loan at the bank for $6,000.00 to help me start this new business independent of the restaurant and motel."

"Maggie, I can loan you the $6,000 at no interest for a year so you could get started."

"Arnold. I have the collateral, and my credit is good at the bank. I don't want your money. What I want from you is more personal, and I want to keep it that way."

"Ah. I understand," Arnold said and eyed the bedroom door.

Maggie pulled him up from the chair, but to his surprise pushed him towards the front door instead of toward the bedroom. She opened the door, leaned up to kiss him, shoved him out into the night, and said, "Tomorrow big guy."

CHAPTER 22

Arnold picked Maggie up in his truck the next morning at 10:00 AM. Maggie had a long list of supplies she planned to order in Pueblo and during the drive she went over the list and prattled happily to Arnold about her optimism.

"I'm going to make good money from this deal for a change," Maggie stated.

"What do you consider 'good money?'" Arnold asked.

"A profit of approximately 20%," Maggie replied.

"I wish you success. It is always exciting to start a new operation. Keep me posted and if you need any help, let me know, but don't let me interfere with your work."

"Arnold. You don't interfere. You give good advice. In fact, come around more often."

They arrived in Pueblo ahead of time and visited several restaurant-supply companies and food wholesalers. Maggie ordered supplies and negotiated to have the supplies delivered in 20 days, and in the future, 20 days after receiving new orders with the same discount applied.

They took a quick break for lunch at a diner that served Mexican food. Maggie was proud of her negotiating and eager to try out her new skills on the suppliers she still had to visit that afternoon.

"I hope I have room for all the extra food in my large refrigerator," Maggie worried aloud as she sipped her coffee.

"Since you have not done this type of thing before, you have to do a lot of guessing without history to go on," Arnold commented.

"Mmmm. That is for sure," Maggie agreed.

In the afternoon, as in the morning, Arnold, went along with Maggie as she looked at silverware, macaroni, and packaged milk. He was a big smiling presence that silently watched to make sure no one took advantage of Maggie.

It was getting dark when they checked into a motel near their last stop. They dropped their luggage in the one room they decided to share and walked across the street to a restaurant that the desk clerk recommended for dinner. The young man had excellent taste it turned out. The thick steaks, huge baked potatoes, and blueberry pie were delicious.

As they left the restaurant, Arnold made a left turn and stopped by the liquor store for a bottle of whiskey and a couple of cups of ice.

Maggie eyed his purchases. "What no wine?"

Arnold's eyebrows went up. With a grin, he turned around and reentered the liquor store. When he came back out, he carried a paper bag with two bottles instead of one and balanced the cups of ice in one hand.

Maggie changed into her night dress as soon as they were in their room and had the door locked.

Arnold sat down on the bed and opened the bottle of whiskey, pouring the amber liquid over the ice cubes in one of the cups. He opened the bottle of wine for Maggie. Maggie poured herself wine in one of the motels coffee cups and scooted up on the bed so her back rested against the headboard.

Arnold took off his boots and socks and unbuttoned his shirt. Maggie studied his flat stomach and the muscles that bulged in his shoulders and arms as he removed the shirt. Arnold glanced over at her and grinned. She sipped her wine and studied him. Still in his jeans, he rested his shoulders against the headboard beside her narrow ones and stretched his long legs out.

They sipped their drinks in silent contentment for some minutes. Arnold thought about the last time they had slept together. It had not all been, sleeping. For a woman almost twice his age, Maggie had a lot of fire in her. They had been in Denver that night. Maggie had been on her way to Israel for a vacation, and her plane had been delayed. Arnold who had driven her to the airport stayed the night with her to make sure she got on the flight the next morning.

Maggie set her cup down on the bedside table and Arnold followed suit. He scooted down in the bed and turned towards her. Maggie followed suit. Arnold reached out and stroked the soft skin of her slender arm. He allowed his hand to keep going, running down the silky fabric of her night dress to its hem. He hooked his fingers around the hem and lifted the fabric, so it folded just below her breasts. He stroked the skin of her thighs and belly and slipped his hand under the night dress to run his finger over her soft breast and tight nipples.

Maggie watched him, her lips parted ever slightly. Her eyes narrowed to slits. Arnold felt Maggie small rough hand begin to explore his belly and chest. It roamed to his belt and fiddled there tapping the metal buckle.

Arnold snickered. "Okay Ma'am."

A wide grin pulled at Maggie's lips.

Arnold threw his long legs over the bed and undressed the rest of the way. He stood for her inspection, his penis enlarging, stretching before her eyes. Maggie swung her legs out of her side of the bed and pulled her night dress over her head. They stared at each other, the bed between their bodies.

Arnold went around the bed and quickly picked her up in his arms. He kissed her lips and then lowered his lips to her breasts, exploring their softness. He laid her down on the bed and pressed his body over hers. She wrapped her arms around his neck and opened her legs around his hips. He reached down and ran his finger around her vagina and guided himself into her, pressing slowly into her hot, tight body. Maggie clung to him and he placed his large hands behind her backside to move her against him, warming them both up, building a quickening rhythm, until his hands and her legs gripped tightly. Their bodies taut, they arched into each other, and both cried out softly as they climaxed.

Arnold tipped over sidewise on the bed taking his weight off Maggie. She rolled with him sleepily.

"It has been a long time Arnold. But it was worth the wait," she whispered and laid her graying head on the pillow. Arnold fell asleep beside her smiling, his arm thrown over her protectively.

Their return trip to Alamos was smooth going. They arrived in time for Maxine to help unload their purchases. While carrying boxes of supplies, Arnold got to know Maxine a little better. He decided she was a great addition to Maggie's staff and would contribute to the newly signed contract work as well.

At the Beth Ranch, Arnold learned that Beth was out of town for an emergency meeting and planned to spend the night and return the next day.

"I am in charge," Shoo Ann said.

Alice arrived soon after Arnold and asked if they were going to eat at the house or at the restaurant

"What is your choice?" Shoo Ann asked.

"If I have to cook, I vote for the restaurant," Alice replied. She turned to Arnold and abruptly grabbed him by his butt and shoved him toward the door. When he returned the favor and grabbed her by her butt, she quickly decided she was in no hurry to eat and they wrestled to the floor.

Alice jumped on Arnold's back and clung. Arnold reached around and grabbed the top of her jeans, pulling her off and on to the floor under him. Soon, Shoo Ann joined in the fray, taking Alice's place on Arnold's back, she playfully bit his ear and tickled his armpits. Arnold gave a great howl and threw them all to the side as he tried to get away from Shoo Ann's fingers. The three of them regrouped laughing, twisting, and turning, hands moving over breasts and butts, armpits, and groins, even feet. They got to laughing so hard they had to stop to catch their breath.

Disheveled, but still dressed, the three decided to eat at the restaurant and have dessert at home.

Beth returned from Pueblo at 11:00 AM. She had dropped all the others in her work group off at their homes before coming home herself. She did not drive into the ranch yard until 3:30 PM. Beth had driven one of the ranch cars and on her way into the house instead of greeting him like she normally would, pointed out to Arnold that the car might need oil. She turned away and took her luggage to the house. She seemed out of sorts to Arnold.

"Did the car run okay?" Arnold asked as he entered the house, following Beth to the room the shared.

"It did." Beth said, continuing to unpack her suitcase.

"What happened? Why did you have to go so abruptly?"

"The problem was resolved."

"I see," Arnold said carefully realizing she was not in a good mood. "I thought you would be home earlier. Sister Mary Teresa called Shoo Ann to say she left her gloves in the car when you dropped the nuns off at around 11:00 this morning," Arnold said.

"All we needed to do was answer some questions raised by some very self-involved parents. I am irritated at them. Sorry to be so grumpy. Those girls will be better off under our care," Beth grumbled and pushed her long hair off her forehead.

Deciding to avoid a possible disagreement, Arnold turned towards the bedroom door, planning to head for the barn and load up some tools to repair fences at the Janell Ranch. The newly named Alamosa Educational and Advancement Home for Homeless Ladies seemed to keep Beth locked in battles to ensure the girls were educated and nourished.

He stopped as Beth called him back, apparently needing an ear.

"Arnold. The attitude of the conservative Catholic nuns makes me so mad. They table all progressive initiatives," Beth said as she closed the empty suitcase and shoved it under the bed.

He heard her frustration and taking her hand started to lead her to the kitchen. He stopped and turned back to Beth and sniffed.

"You smell like sex, like semen. Where have you been since you dropped off the nuns?"

Beth pulled away from him and went into the kitchen where she poured him and herself a cup of coffee.

Beth looked into her coffee cup and not at Arnold.

"I ran into Mark at Maggie's. We talked."

Arnold's eyes narrowed. He was listening intently and took a sip of his coffee.

"Jerry is still around you know," Beth continued. "He was hired by a rancher down the road after you made me fire him. He thought it was very unfair that you would have him fired when he did nothing wrong. I am still upset about it too. This is my ranch and I should decide who to fire and who to hire. I am thinking of hiring Jerry back."

Arnold set his cup down and sat up straighter, alert.

"You didn't consult me on that? How often do you meet with Jerry, Beth?"

"I see him every now and then."

"Is Jerry why you smell like sex?"

"That is none of your business."

"Will you bring Jerry here? I'd like to hear more about this job you are going to hire him to perform."

Beth called Jerry and an hour later, Jerry walked into the living room of the ranch house.

Pointing to the cowboy, Beth said, "Arnold, you remember Jerry Miller. He worked here."

Jerry's face was tense as was Beth's and Arnold. Jerry and Arnold did not shake hands.

"I have some questions about these meetings you and Beth have been having at Maggie's motel. To get straight, to the point. Did you and Beth have sex today in a motel room?"

"Yes, we did," Jerry replied.

Beth got up and left the room.

"How many times did you and Beth have sexual intercourse?" Arnold demanded.

Jerry's face was rigid. "Today? Oh, five or six times."

Arnold felt his face get red. "Did you and she engage in oral sex too?"

Jerry replied, "Yes we both did on each other."

Beth had returned to the living room right before Jerry answered that last question. She looked horrified.

"Beth, you know exactly how serious this matter is to our relationship," Arnold growled, not forgetting but not counting the fact that he had spent the night before with Maggie in a Pueblo motel, and not only sleeping.

"Did you hear my question to Jerry? Did you hear his answer?" Arnold shouted.

Beth started to cry. "Yes, I heard both."

"Were his answers correct?" Arnold hammered on.

Beth sobbed out, "Yes."

Arnold felt himself sicken as rage swept through him. He struggled to control himself.

"There is nothing more insulting to a me, or any man, than to learn his loved one has allowed another man to penetrate her vagina. Now I have learned that this occurred willingly five or six times today."

Arnold swung back so he was looking in Jerry's direction. He said, "Jerry, you insinuated that Beth has been having sex with you more than just today. Is that correct?"

Jerry raised his chin as if preparing for a blow. "Yes. We have had sex several times. If you were going to fire me for something I did not do, I figured I might as well do it and be guilty."

Arnold took one step toward Jerry but stopped.

"I suggest that after today you and I should never meet at any time for any reason. Right now, I am so mad I might kill you."

"Beth. I will be packing my belongings at once. I'll be gone from your ranch within 24 hours. I am sorry our relationship, our engagement to be married, had to terminate in this ugly manner."

Arnold looked at his watch. It was 4:00 PM. He turned on his boot heal and left Jerry and Beth standing in the living room. He got into his truck and went to the Alamosa bank and cancelled existing and all future support for the Alamosa Educational and Advancement Home. He canceled all support and financial connections he had to Beth's or Janell's ranch operations or expenses incurred therefrom.

The banker was extremely upset.

"No! This will stop everything. The project will be broke! He yelled.

"Tell your problems to Jerry and Beth or the Catholic Church." Arnold replied coldly.

CHAPTER 23

When Arnold arrived back at the Beth Ranch after terminating his association with the Alamosa Bank and the Home for Girls, he entered the ranch house and slammed the door. No one was about. Shoo Ann and Alice must have been hiding in their bedroom. He packed his clothing in the same bag he had brought with him back from Oklahoma and drug it out to the truck. He tossed it in the back.

Next Arnold backed up to his horse trailer and hitched it onto the truck. In the barn, he loaded up hay for Black Shadow and filled the traveling water barrel he used to make sure the horse had water when traveling.

Shoo Ann appeared in the runway of the barn.

"Arnold. Not again. You can't leave us again."

"Shoo Ann, I can."

"Beth is in the kitchen pulling her hair out. She keeps saying. 'I knew this would happen.'"

Arnold did not respond. He gathered up Black Shadow's tack and put everything but the lead rope into the horse trailer's storage.

"Forgive her, Arnold. Sex is no big deal. You have it with me and Alice. Beth has it with me and Alice. Cool down."

Jerry entered the barn too.

"I have something I want to say. This is entirely my fault. I was so angry that you had Beth fire me because she was or might become attracted to me when I loved this job so much, I swore I would get even with you. I was the aggressor while in bed. During our times in bed, Beth would say that she was committing the worst sin she had ever thought of and was asking God for forgiveness even before we had stopped having sex with each other."

"Did you continue to perform oral sex on Beth while she was asking God to forgive her?"

Jerry stared at his boots.

Arnold took that as a 'Yes.'

"Mark, I acknowledge that Beth is a fabulous, beautiful and tremendous woman deserving of care, love and support. I have loved Beth and had planned to care and support her forever. Unfortunately, tonight, my relationship with Beth was destroyed by you and your actions. I hope you are a man who can live up to the challenges that lay ahead for both of you. Now, please leave and do not let me see you again."

Jerry looked like he wanted to say more but spun on his heel and left. Alice, who was sticking her head in the barn door but had not come all the way in, pulled it back as Jerry brushed by her.

Arnold paced, trying to collect his thoughts and Shoo Ann sat dejected on a bale of hay, Alice ran to Arnold and threw her arms around his waist.

"Arnold this is the saddest day of my life. I have, in these short three months, grown to love you more than any individual alive today, except Shoo Ann, so please give Beth another chance."

Arnold stood frozen; Alice's slim arms were tight around his waist.

"Let go of me Alice," Arnold said quietly. She did and he retrieved Black Shadow's saddle and halter from the horse trailer, threw two blankets into the saddle bag and swung up onto the stallion's back.

To get away from everyone, Arnold traveled to his favorite place on the ranch. He slept while Black Shadow stood guard. It was cool when he awakened at 2:00 AM. He pulled a second blanket from its place behind the saddle and wrapped it around his shoulders. He mounted Black Shadow and they walked across the ranch in the darkness, west, then south then back toward the barn. It was 4:30 AM. He saw that there was a light on in the ranch house, but he did not go up.

He unsaddled Black Shadow and stowed his tack in the horse trailer once again. He was checking the hitch when Beth approached him. He did not say anything.

Beth shrugged. "I was sleeping in the hay waiting for you."

"I wanted to be near you again," She continued. "I feel such sorrow and shame. I know you feel sorrow too. I think we can deal with it better together, than separately."

Arnold felt worn and empty. "Perhaps you are right," he acknowledged, gesturing toward the rumpled blanket bed that Beth had been sleeping on. It was still dark and cold outside.

"Let's rest and not talk for a while."

They lay down in the bed on the hay, hugged each other, put a blanket over themselves and went to sleep.

Arnold dreamed God was talking to him, God and his Father, God rest his soul. He could not tell in his dream who was talking to Beth, but it was probably, God, Shoo Ann, and Alice. He was still listening trying to understand when he woke and found Beth lying beside him sound asleep and Black Shadow and Autumn Time looking down at them.

He woke Beth.

"I'll saddle the horses if you'll get some coffee and extra blankets," his voice was rough, used up from emotion and sleeping in the cool air.

After the horses were saddle, Arnold grabbed his trusty 30-06 for comfort. Beth joined him with a thermos of coffee. In the morning light, he could see that she was pale, her eyes were puffy from crying.

Without saying anything, they rode away from the ranch. The cool breeze seemed to encourage clear thinking.

Arnold knew that everyone at the ranch wanted them to stay together. Their mounts rode close together, as if they too, shared the popular opinion. For his part, Arnold was struggling. The hurt of 12 years had come roaring back with a vengeance causing him to feel sick to his stomach. Images of Jerry having sex with Beth and penetrating her vagina beat around in his head. He did not know what to do.

Reaching the tall trees, green grass, flowers and flowing brook of their favorite place on the whole ranch, the horses stopped on their own, and the riders dismounted. Arnold spread a blanket over the grass for warmth. He sat down on it and helped Beth down beside him. He then told Beth, "I am forgiving you for having sex with Jerry. I am not, at this time, willing to go through with our wedding."

Before he could finish his statement, tears had started to pour out of his eyes. Beth's eyes filled and overflowed. The two sat there next to the stream, next to each other, crying for a long time.

Beth asked, "If we are not going through with the wedding, what should I do with the ring?"

"Did you wear it when you made love to Jerry?"

"Yes," Beth whispered, I forgot to remove it."

A spark of anger rekindled in Arnold's tired brain, "Then, keep it so you can wear it again when Jerry is with you in the future."

"That is mean of you to say," Beth wailed. "I cannot endure such thoughts."

"There is no reason for you to wear it now. Keep it in its box until you decide what to do with it. I no longer care."

Beth wrapped her arms around Arnold and held him as tight as she could. She looked into his eyes.

"Either, I am forgiven, or I'm not. It cannot be halfway. I won't endure remarks that hurt."

Arnold stared back but did not respond.

"To be honest," Beth continued, "I feel the need for sexual satisfaction very often and the need is urgent. I have tried to satisfy this need with you and Shoo Ann. When neither of you are available, I begin to panic. That is what happened with Jerry. That is why I wanted your permission to be with him sometimes."

"Do you have deep feelings of love or even affection for Jerry?" Arnold asked curtly.

Beth said, "No. I just needed sexual satisfaction and a lot of it. I don't know how to deal with the situation."

"I was here and fully capable of meeting your needs," Arnold responded.

"Not when you are in Oklahoma."

Before Arnold could say anything to that, Beth continued.

"Something else. I learned from my doctor and the surgeon that I would forever experience the effects of hormonal imbalances. These cause me to have periods of insatiable appetite for sexual stimulation."

Beth took a deep breath and went on.

"When we have sex, you and I, I do not want you to stop, even after an hour or so. I want you to experience more than one orgasm or climax, and I want you to be active inside me to arouse me fully. I enjoy the experience and want it to last a long time or to be repeated multiple times, sometimes in the vagina and sometimes in the anus and sometimes both. I think my expectations are excessive and confused. I did not talk to you about it because I am afraid you will not understand."

"I Remember your doctor saying something about this and your hormone levels after your operation," Arnold said. "He said we must learn to deal with it. I wonder if we can coordinate our schedules. There cannot be another event such as the one that just occurred with Jerry. Let me emphasize, there cannot be another event like the one that just occurred."

"You want to talk more about Jerry and I?" asked Beth.

"Yes. You said that you did not have feelings toward him."

"That is correct. I have no feelings for Jerry other than sexual attraction and an acknowledgment that he is a very good cowboy with good horse sense, and furthermore I did not have those feelings when we had sex yesterday. I merely needed sex over and over again. When that feeling comes to me again, I will need the same thing, and I will feel the same way. I will need sex over and over again."

"I'm sorry I am interrupting, but it is important to me to know that this will not happen again with Jerry or any man," Arnold insisted.

"I want you to forgive me because I want you to stay with me. You are the only man who has ever satisfied me and made me enjoy one maybe two orgasms and feel completely satisfied. To be perfectly clear, you are the only man I have ever had sexual intercourse with besides Jerry. Jerry does not know how to satisfy a woman; he knows nothing and is unable to do what needs to be done. You know what is required and are totally able to provide it."

"I am flattered, but can I trust you to be true to me?" Arnold asked.

"Yes. I know now. It had not occurred to me before the situation with Jerry, that I could not control myself," Beth admitted.

Beth looked into his eyes and said, "Sweetheart I am sorry. I have thought of your hurt, the hurt you feel now and the one you will carry with you for the rest of your life. I feel it too. I hurt painfully and wish it would just go away. I committed a sin that God has not yet forgiven. I know that what I did was wrong, and I did it anyway, and I alone will carry that burden until you and God forgive me."

Arnold returned her embrace. "Someday it will happen," he said. "Beth, I have already forgiven you. God will soon."

They sat for a while in silence and then as the sun rose higher in the sky, they got up, folded the blanket, remounted, and rode back to the barn. They unsaddled the horses and walked side by side to the house.

As they entered the living room, Beth gave Arnold another hug and they went to the kitchen and fixed themselves breakfast.

As they finished eating, the phone rang. Arnold answered it. Charlie Anderson was on the other end of the line, telling him to sit down he had some sad news.

Arnold braced himself, unable to imagine what Charlie might have to say.

"I'll just come right out and say it. Alex and her two daughters have been killed in an accident involving her pick-up and a cement truck delivering cement to your new house. They died instantly and were not recognizable when rescued by the police and fire department. The concrete was for the roads and sidewalks around the house. For some reason, the concrete truck driver crossed the center line at high speed and hit Alex and her girls head on."

"Oh God!" Arnold cried out.

"I'll let you know when the services will be scheduled," Charlie said. "I don't think it will be right away because many of her relatives lived out of state."

Arnold hung up the phone, sat down and wept.

Beth came running out of the kitchen. "What has happened?"

He could not talk. He waved Beth away and went out the door. He went straight to the barn and climbed on Black Shadow. He rode away alone.

He thought God was telling him that sometimes the price you must pay for forgiveness is very high.

Arnold rode for an hour or so and then he went back to Beth and told her what happened.

The next morning, Arnold called Charlie back.

"I'm sorry I didn't ask before. How are you handling Alex's death?" Arnold asked.

Charlie's voice was raw. It sounded as if he had been crying. "I cannot talk about it," Charlie said. "I'll have my secretary call you."

Within minutes the phone rang, and it was Charlie's secretary on the line. "The funeral and services will be next Wednesday at the Calumet Red Rock United Methodist Church at 10:00 AM." Arnold tried to say something, but nothing came out, and he hung up the phone after listening to the woman's message. Later he called and apologized to Charlie's secretary.

CHAPTER 24

Arnold was grieving. He seemed to age a decade in less than a day. His walk had slowed, and he lost his train of thought easily, returning to a room multiple times, trying to remember what he was looking for. He knew Beth could not really understand. She had only met Alex once while in Oklahoma.

The next morning, Beth approached him about the financial support for the home for girls.

"David Baker from the Alamos Bank called this morning and wants to know how we are going to proceed with the home for girls following the events of the other day."

Arnold asked Beth, "Do you have time to go to the bank with me right now?"

She replied, "Yes."

At the bank in Alamos, they were welcomed by David. As they sat in his office, he wanted to know how to proceed with payment of notes coming due. Beth asked for the total of all of them plus those expected to be due within thirty days. The total equaled over seventeen thousand dollars and her own current balance was less than a hundred dollars. She looked at Arnold.

"Restore the banking arrangement we had before yesterday. You will be able to meet the expenses."

David looked elated. Beth looked at Arnold concerned. "Are you sure?"

"Yes," Arnold replied ruefully. "There are times when my temper gets in my way of doing business and what is right."

The banker scrambled to reassemble the papers for Arnold to sign again.

As they went out the door, Beth smiled, hugged his arm, and gestured with her thumb toward the banker, "I think he is happier than anybody, except me."

Arnold was not so sure as Beth of his own happiness. He continued to think about Jerry and Beth — in bed on the drive back to the Beth ranch from Alamosa.

I must face the fact, Arnold thought to himself, neither Charlene nor Beth were true to me.

Why? Was it a shortage of money? Was ego on the ladies' part or mine part of the problem? Was it sexual? Arnold did not think so. He seemed to satisfy the ladies sexually. He was attentive to their needs and big where it counted. There were times when he received, what he thought were great positive comments about his sexual prowess.

Arnold began to equate sex and his duties on the ranch. He decided he should clarify this with Beth. Beth had hired two men to help her and maybe she did not need him anymore. Was Jerry going to be a replacement for him while the two hired hands took care of the ranch?

Watching the road while he drove, Arnold asked, "Beth, since you now have two people hired to help you perform work on the ranch and you have people you know, such as Jerry to provide needed sexual satisfaction, do you consider me no longer necessary? Is this the reason you were not true to me?"

Beth sighed. She simply said, "No."

"I don't understand then what is the reason?"

"As the surgeon and my physician said, I could expect to encounter periods when I would need significant sexual attention to meet my needs and the reason for this is hormonal. To avoid a recurrence of what happened with Jerry, you and I need to be together. You need to be available when I get an insatiable urge. When that happens, you get to enjoy me for as long as you like."

Arnold sat in silence for a moment.

"I want to believe you. However, I get nervous when you say that I have to be present when the hormones hit. If I am not present will you look for Jerry or some other man who is ready and willing? You are a beautiful and desirable woman. You can easily find a man who could serve your purpose. I'm sorry but my head is consumed with complications and fears. We have a serious problem Beth. I believe you would do your best to resist temptation; however, according to your surgeon and your doctor, your best may not be enough. I have lost my trust in you. I simply cannot get the picture of the two of you having sexual intercourse and also oral sex out of his mind. The image affects me when you and I are having sex."

They had arrived at the Beth ranch by then. Beth got out of the truck and look sadly at Arnold. She came around the truck and hugged him. They walked slowly to the house. Arnold was feeling like a chump, thinking this was a place where he no longer belonged.

He asked Beth, "Do you want me to stay or leave?"

"I want you to stay. You are important to me," she cried. "Please be calm and everything will be okay." They went to bed and he tossed and turned, unable to sleep, unable to rest, unable to think clearly. The picture of Jerry and Beth haunted him. Beth lay close to him and remained awake, not saying a word. After a couple of hours, she got out of bed and listened to the radio. That didn't help because the sound irritated Arnold, so she returned to the bed.

Beth sat beside him in bed with tears streaming from her eyes, "Arnold, what do you want me to do? Is there anything I can do to correct what I have has done? I am sorry for my mistakes and I will forever be sorry; I can say out loud the things you said I did with Jerry and then genuinely apologize again; would that help? Only God can help both of us, you to forget and me to forever be true to you."

"Beth I am hurting beyond comprehension and when I talk, the wrong words come out of my mouth, so I do not want to talk and hurt you more. I am leaving. I need time away."

Arnold swung his long legs out of the bed. He dressed in the dark and went to the barn. Most of what he owned was still packed. He refreshed Black Shadows supplies, hung the stallions tack in the trailer and checked the trailer hitch. All was ready. He swung into the seat on the driver's side of the truck and turned the key. The engine roared.

The porch light at the ranch house came on as he drove down the lane. He could see Beth standing there in her night gown and robe.

As he drove by, she held up two cups of coffee. He guessed that she expected him to stop for a good cup of coffee, but this time, he did not.

Arnold drove down the road from the Beth Ranch a couple of miles and then pulled over when he had enough room to get off the winding road safely. His eyes were full of tears and he could hardly see. His stomach was upset. He buried his face in his hands and let the tears flow. He sat there by the side of the road for all of a half hour hoping no one he knew would pull up and want to talk. Black Shadow shifted in the trailer uneasily.

Arnold drove on, unsure of his destination.

Arnold began looking for a place to stop where he could board Black Shadow and find space for himself. He knew such a place might not be easy to find. He was tired already from all the emotion of the last days, and he hurt from one end of his body to the other. He still felt nauseous and thought he might vomit. He continued to drive looking for a stable where he could feed, water, and exercise Black Shadow. He found a likely establishment called the Horseshoe Stable and stopped. The attendant told him the price for the horse was $25.00 per night. The cost for horse and person was $50.00 with supper and breakfast included. He paid the money and unloaded Black Shadow from the trailer. He turned the stallion out into the pasture that had a shelter. He was the only horse there. He set out hay and checked that the shelter had water. Black Shadow wandered off inspecting the new location.

Arnold settled into a tiny room and thought.

At first, he was sure he was heading for Oklahoma. Then, he realized that he wanted to see Brenda again. He had not talked to Brenda for a long time, but he could picture her like it was yesterday, standing in the doorway of her father's ranch house. She was tall. Her reddish hair glinted gold in the sun, and long it curled down over her shoulders. The last time he had looked into her dark blue eyes, they had been sad, sad and silent, mourning the death of her father.

She would understand his sorrow.

Arnold called Brenda from the phone in the room.

She answered.

"Arnold. I'm so glad to hear from you. Where are you? How are you? You have been on my mind for days now."

Arnold was so surprised she answered, he was speechless for a few seconds. It was stunning to hear her clear voice again.

"Hello Brenda. I can't see you, but your voice is lovely as ever," he said finally. "Do you object if I come and visit you?"

"Object! I don't object. I'd like to see you, right now if possible," she replied.

"I'm on my way then. It looks like you are staying in the same hotel. I can find you there. I should be there tomorrow midday."

"I can't wait to see you and talk about all that we have missed together. And Arnold, the Chaplin is long gone."

Arnold checked on Black Shadow one more time then he laid down in his narrow bunkhouse bed and sensing an upbeat and cheerful spirit surrounding him, he drifted to sleep with a smile, his heartbreak over Beth already fading in the prospect of seeing Brenda again.

CHAPTER 25

Arnold awoke early. After feeling almost ill the day before, he was amazed that he felt well rested. It seemed as if his decision to see Brenda was giving him a new lease on life. He went up to the main house for breakfast and coffee, glad the meal was part of his room rent. He told the proprietor that he was heading out and thanked him for the place to stay for the night.

After loading Black Shadow into the trailer, Arnold headed east, planning to turn north to Denver at Walsenburg. It was 8:30 AM. He expected to get into Denver right after lunch.

It felt right to him to be going to Brenda. He never really had planned to leave her. Her relationship with the Chaplain at the hospital where her father had died had concerned Arnold so much that he had assumed the worst and left. Brenda refused to say anything about her relationship with the chaplain. Despite Arnold's questions, she neither confirmed nor denied that their relationship was romantic or sexual. She would just look at him, her lip turned down stubbornly, leaving him to think what he liked.

Of course, what he thought, he did not like. He remembered Brenda as a virgin. She had been eager for sexual experience, responsive to his lovemaking, but totally naive. She was very attractive and very natural. It was hard for him to imagine that any man who spent time with her would not want to make love to her, marry her, and wrap her up and keep her safe. And, it was hard for him to imagine her saying, "No."

Arnold stopped in Colorado Springs for a black cup of coffee, and he gave Black Shadow a drink of water.

Brenda was staying in a hotel on the southern side of Denver, not too far into the city. Arnold planned to stop at a stable as he neared town and find a place for Black Shadow to safely run while he drove on to the hotel and Brenda. He passed a sign for Cloud View Stables and Horse Boarding. It was located in a lovely valley just off the road. He turned around as soon as he could and went back. He rented a stable and pasture for Black Shadow for a day. While he was in the office, he borrowed the phone to call Brenda and let her know that he was less than an hour away.

"I'll be back tomorrow old Boy," Arnold said as he turned Black Shadow out into the corral. He fed him some oats from the palm of his hand, patted the strong warm neck and chest, and ran his hands down each of the stallion's legs making sure he had no injuries from trailering. Then, he unhitched the horse trailer and turned away to get back on the road, knowing his horse had good water and room to roam.

Arnold knocked on the door numbered 6. Brenda answered on the first knock. For a second, they stood there one on the inside and one on the outside, taking each other in, cataloging the changes. Arnold noticed that there were a couple of tiny lines around Brenda's eyes that had not been there before. Her cheeks may have been a bit hollower than he remembered, and her red-blonde hair was cut in a straight line at her shoulders and not curling wildly in every direction. She looked as beautiful as ever. Her deep blue eyes were traveling over him from head to toe.

He towered over her in the doorway. Arnold was 31 years old now. His hair was still dark and curly, shaped by the cowboy hat he held in his hand. He was still a sizeable man, but perhaps a bit thinner than he had been when she last saw him 2 years ago. There was the slightest hint of grey in his whiskers now. He had not shaved that morning. His face was tanned, wind burned, and lined. His deep blue eyes sparkled, and a smile was creeping over his mouth. Arnold definitely took up space.

Brenda stepped back, inviting him into her room.

Arnold surveyed the room. It was the same, but more lived in now. Brenda had been living in this room since he left her two years ago. The last time they had made love it was on this bed.

"May I hug you Brenda?"

"Yes! Yes! I thought you would never ask," Brenda squeaked. She threw herself into his arms and wrapped hers around his back squeezing tight.

"I am so glad to see you," she whispered into his shirt front.

Arnold rested his face in her hair and smiled, smelling the sweet rose and lavender scent of her. He rocked her back and forth. After a while he kissed the top of her head, then her cheek. Then, his lips moved on top of hers and he kissed her for real and she kissed him back with all the passion he remembered so well.

Arnold had not really expected to fall right into bed with Brenda, but that is what he did. They kept kissing and moved over to the bed. Arnold remembered to kick the hotel room door shut before they actually made it to the bed. Brenda giggled against his lips.

Arnold lifted Brenda and dropped her onto the bed, following her down. His lips began to travel, relearning the feel and taste of Brenda's lips, chin, cheeks, eyes, brow, and neck. He took hungry little bites of each part of her he found.

Brenda's long fingers clung to his shoulders. When he looked down at her, he saw a serene smile on her face. She reached up and kissed his unshaven face. Her warm kisses moved to his neck, along his jaw to his ear. He pulled away from her because it tickled.

"Shall we undress or have a tickle fight?" Arnold asked huskily, his forehead resting on hers. He ran his fingers over her ribs. She squirmed and laughed. "I'm pretty sure I'd win, Arnold laughed.

"I say, let's undress," gasped Brenda.

They rolled off the bed and stepped away from each other. Brenda reached for her shirt buttons and smiled up into Arnold's eyes as she undid them one by one. Arnold started to undo his own shirt, but he kept getting distracted and stopping to watch Brenda's skin being slowly revealed.

He reached one large finger and ran it down from the hollow at the base of her neck, over her breastbone, through her cleavage to where her fingers had come to a stop frozen on the buttons.

Arnold's mind lost all thought as his knuckles ran over the inside curves of Brenda's breasts. Her skin was so smooth. His hands moved to push the shirt down over her shoulders just as Brenda managed to undo the last button. Her shirt fell to the floor.

Brenda moved to unbutton the last of Arnold's shirt buttons. She reached up and pressing her breasts to his naked chest pushed his shirt off his shoulders. Arnold had to shrug to get the shirt completely off.

With her arms around his neck and her breasts pressed to his chest, Brenda looked into Arnold's eyes, hers warm and smiling.

Arnold's hands moved over Brenda's waist and undid her jeans. He pushed his hands down over her buttock, removing fabric as he went. Brenda worked to unbutton his jeans. He stood patiently while she worked the zipper down over the bulge that had risen there. His breathing got heavier.

When she slipped her hands inside and tried to push the tight jeans down over his hip bones, Arnold stepped back and pushed them down himself. Now that they were both mostly naked, Arnold moved closer again, and Brenda grasped his penis in her hands.

Arnold gritted his teeth with pleasure as her hands moved over his bared flesh.

Daylight poured into the room and Arnold's eyes were glued to the pale circle of skin that surrounded the tight coral-colored knot of her nipple. His hands followed his eyes, and he caressed her the tight nubs with his rough thumbs. Brenda's hands moved to Arnold's hips and explored the hard muscles of his thighs, moving onto his buttock.

Their eyes locked together. Arnold swung Brenda up into his arms and deposited her on the bed again, following her down. He lay on his side facing her. His big hand spread out over her stomach.

"Arnold. That makes me ache deep down inside." Brenda whispered.

Arnold quirked his eyebrow in query and added a little more pressure then slid his fingers down, down into the curly hair that covered her pubis. His fingers explored and caressed. Her body flushed pink before his eyes, and she arched her hips off the bed. He dropped his head down to suckle gently at her breast. She cried out and spread her legs wide in welcome.

Arnold answered the invitation. He rolled over on her and drove himself into the tight recesses of her body. She was so hot around him.

Arnold watched Brenda's eyes become slits. Her breathing quickened. Her neck arched back as Arnold pressed deep inside her. Arnold's own breathing became harsh. Their bodies moved together, slowly at first and then faster until Brenda climaxed with a shudder and Arnold followed her, releasing his sperm in one hard thrust that he held deep inside her heat. He could feel the tiny quivers of Brenda's body tight around him.

For a few minutes he stayed where he was, his weight pressing her into the mattress. Then, he rolled back. He reached over to the far side of the bed where a patchwork quilt sat waiting to be put in a drawer. He shook it open and laid in over their cooling bodies. He pulled a pillow out from under the bed spread and settled it beneath Brenda's head as she smiled up at him drowsily. He laid his head beside hers on the pillow and whispered, "Home."

He fell into a deep satisfied sleep.

When he woke, Brenda was watching him quietly. The sun had moved farther into the west and shown in window. Brenda's hair was riotous and glistened in the gold light.

Arnold stretched and leaned over to give Brenda a quick kiss. He suggested they shower and go somewhere to eat and talk.

Of course, the shower for two took a lot longer than a shower for one. The hot water ran out and they had to get down to the business of washing as the warm water went to cool and then to darn fight cold.

"Ah! Ah! Let's get out of here," Brenda whooped.

Arnold laughed and getting out reached back for her with a big fluffy towel. He wrapped her in it and then set about drying himself.

They found a restaurant only a block away that offered steaks, salads, and rolls. They slid into a booth, and Arnold ordered coffee immediately. Brenda ordered coffee too.

"I remember you loved your coffee. Arnold."

"Yep. Something don't change."

"My Dad loved his coffee too." Brenda remembered. She smiled at the thought.

"I sure wish Henry had lived longer so I could have gotten to know him better."

"He was so happy you were there Arnold. He felt relief knowing you were there to pick up where he left off. You did a good job taking care of things," Brenda said.

"Well I don't feel like I'm done with that yet. Brenda, would you consider coming home with me to Oklahoma? I brand new house that I haven't even lived in and lots of land. My finances are great too. Remember I told you I had investments."

"I don't really have a plan for my life. Arnold," Brenda signed. "I've just been setting here, living day to day since father died and you left."

"What about the Chaplain?" Arnold blurted out.

"What about him?" Brenda asked.

"Why didn't you marry him?"

"I don't love him. I never loved him."

"Did you have sex with him?" Arnold could have smacked himself for asking, but he couldn't help himself.

"Arnold. I am not talking about my private life. I've said this before. Brenda scolded. "You either trust me or you don't. I am not providing any details. The Chaplain tried to help me spiritually after father died. He did help me. Now he is gone, reassigned to someone else."

Arnold frowned down at his hands, trying to take "No" for an answer.

"Well, will you come with me to Oklahoma. I mean live with me. I mean marry me!"

"Arnold?"

"I can't very well ask you to live with me in sin."

"But you just met me again. You hardly know me."

"I know you Brenda, and since the first time I laid eyes on you, I've loved you. I was so relieved to know you were Henry's daughter not his Sweetheart. I remember how my heart froze within me thinking you were his wife." Arnold could not believe he was saying this, but as the words came out of his mouth, he knew it was true.

"I did say I wanted to have your children."

"Yes! You did. That means you love me."

"I guess it does. You always try to do what is right. I admire that. Arnold. I'll go to Oklahoma with you, see your new home, marry you, and build a family with you."

"Thank you," He said. "Thank you."

Arnold sat silently for a while, dumbfounded how much things had changed since yesterday. Yesterday, he had no hope. Today, he had hope. Yesterday he was desolate. Today, he was overjoyed. His Lord and Savior Jesus Christ was standing beside him today and blessing him mightily, more than he deserved.

A huge sound built up in him. He jumped up from the booth grabbed Brenda by the hand and hauled her out of the booth. He picked her up and whirled her around.

"Whoop! Whoop!" he yelled.

CHAPTER 26

Arnold stepped outside of his new home. He noticed the air was cool and light, the sun was bright and warm. His mood was perfect.

He and Brenda had married this morning in a small Methodist ceremony in Calumet. Right now, they were surrounded by a few last neighbors and friends who had come to their party to warm their new home and celebrate their marriage. Each of the guests wished Brenda and Arnold happiness and requested they visit periodically. As the newly married couple stood with their arms around each other in their doorway, they waved their guests off as each departed.

He thought of the long ride from Denver to Calumet with Brenda by his side and Black Shadow in the trailer behind. Brenda had been awed by Black Shadow when he first introduced them.

"He is beautiful!" she had whispered to herself as she and Arnold leaned on the fence at the Cloud View Stables. Black Shadow ran from one side of the pasture to the other throwing his heals up in empty bucks. The cool wind tossed his mane and tail. Arnold was pretty sure he was showing off for Brenda.

Finally, Black Shadow had gotten all the excess energy out of him and wandered up to the fence so Arnold could rub him down. The stallion had eyed Brenda with interest. Arnold had put on his halter on him and led him into the trailer where he gave him a bag of hay to munch on during the drive to Oklahoma. The drive would have been a long one to make all at once so in order not to kill his horse or his girl, he had stopped in Hays, Kansas for a night. That was a week ago. He and Brenda had married this morning in a small Methodist ceremony.

He thought of his parents. He wished they had lived long enough to meet Brenda and participate in their life, be grandparents to the children they hoped to conceive. He knew his father would be happy that he had turned around and come home after leaving Oklahoma without a plan. This move seemed to fulfill his father's wish that he "always do what is right."

Brenda and Arnold found themselves in their new home alone as husband and wife. This reality still surprised them. When finally, alone, they hugged and kissed and danced around the mostly empty house. About the time they were starting to get seriously involved in their kissing, there was a knock at the front door. Upon opening the door, Arnold recalled they had a delivery scheduled for a king-sized bed, dresser, bedside tables, and lamps. When Arnold had ordered it, he thought he was ordering everything a couple would need to furnish a bedroom. Now, he remembered sheets, quilts, and pillows. Brenda said not to worry and made a list.

Once the huge bed was installed, Brenda exclaimed, "So that is what a king size bed is." Arnold laughed and threw her onto the bed. They wrestled for a kiss or two, laughing as they played like two kids, something they enjoyed because they had never played this way before.

Before they got too carried away, they decided to go to El Reno and buy the supplies they needed, including the list of things the bedroom was missing.

As evening approached and they had their supplies put away, put on, or hung up, Arnold stared out the upstairs window and admitted to himself that he was almost as excited about getting Black Shadow a place to call home as he was about having his own home finished.

"Brenda, would you want to purchase a quarter horse mare of your own so you can ride around the farm with me?"

"I would love that Arnold. It has been a long time since I've ridden, at least a couple of years, I miss it."

Arnold called Charlie and asked, him if he knew anyone who raised quarter horses that might want to sell a young mare.

"I was expecting that question," Charlie said. "I saw how you looked at that stallion out in the barn off and on all day. I have done some research. I have found two places that raise and sell quarter horses."

He gave Arnold the phone numbers and recommended his preference based on his knowledge of horses.

"Do you want to accompany Brenda and I when we go to purchase the horse?

"I'd be honored." Charlie replied.

"She wants a black horse the color of Black Shadow only a mare, one that is trained to ride and would be ready to mate in a year so she can have a foal to raise. Brenda would like to train the foal herself."

"Okay. Let's meet at Hamilton's horse farm tomorrow at 10:00 AM."

The next morning as they got out of the truck at Hamilton's horse farm, Brenda became excited and wanted everyone to hurry. The three of them introduced themselves to Mr. Hamilton, and he was very friendly. He told them everything he could remember about each of the five quarter horse mares he had for sale. He had a fact sheet on each one and gave Brenda a copy.

Brenda looked at each horse and asked questions and studied the fact sheet for each. She selected one that looked almost the same color as Black Shadow.

"How old is she? When can she be bred? What training she had received? Brenda asked Mr. Hamilton.

Mr. Hamilton replied, "She is one and a half years of age. She is trained to be a cattle cutting pony and broken to ride. She will be ready to mate within a year."

Brenda asked Arnold and Charlie if they thought the horse she chose, was the best one. They all agreed she made a great choice.

"Her name is Beautiful Sunshine," Mr. Hamilton explained. "She is a registered quarter horse with papers. I will certify the registration for you when you make the purchase."

"I have papers for Black Shadow, so we are in luck," said Arnold.

A month passed without as much as a disagreement between them. It was truly a happy home. Brenda was happy equipping the kitchen. Sexually, she openly expressed her feelings and curiosity to Arnold. Periodically, her questions surprised him, but he enjoyed each one. It was obvious Brenda had led a sheltered life.

Her largest adjustment was getting used to Arnold's investments. They were now hers too. The amounts were scary and caused Brenda to ask a lot of questions. Arnold was not certain she understood everything they discussed, but she was impressed with Arnold's knowledge of business and asked Arnold when she should transfer her money to his account.

"Anytime is good, just be sure to do it before either of us get down to zero dollars," he joked.

Taking him completely seriously, Brenda said, "I will do that." Then she saw the ornery twinkle in his eye and added, "I had better make the transfer now since I intend to spend many dollars tomorrow and I don't want us to run out of money."

That afternoon Arnold received a phone call from Shoo Ann.

"Arnold, I need to talk to you, and it is extremely important."

"Hello Shoo Ann. This is as good a time as any."

"It's about Beth. She is in the hospital in Colorado Springs and she needs to talk to you. She has not eaten since you left the house. She cries constantly and has periodically told me and Alice to leave her alone. She has not seen Jerry since you and he had your conflict either. She does not speak of Jerry at all, only you. I want you to talk to her as it is a life or death matter."

Arnold said, "Okay. I will talk to her. What is her phone number?" Shoo Ann gave it to him, and then she wanted to know if she could give Beth Arnold's number, and he agreed. He promised Shoo Ann that he would call Beth immediately.

He dialed Beth's phone. He let the phone ring twice and Beth answered.

"Hello Beth. How are you doing?"

Beth recognized his voice and said, "Ah Arnold. I do not feel well but I wanted to talk with you, so please do not hang up."

"I called you Beth. I will not hang up. Relax and talk to me," Arnold said.

In between gasps and sniffling noises that let Arnold know she was crying, she said, "Arnold I am as sorry as I can be for what I did. I cannot seem to get you out of my mind, and I know I am the one who did wrong. Will you forgive me? I think that will help. I do not know where you are or what you are doing but I am worried sick, literally sick. I am in the hospital and they have me on intravenous feeding as I have lost weight and am down to 80 pounds. I no longer have a butt or breasts. Will you please say you forgive me?"

"Beth, I have forgiven you and do not worry about me. I am living a peaceful existence. I cannot resume our courtship, but I am not angry with you and I still love you."

"Can you come and see me?"

"I don't have plans to visit you, but that could change in the future."

"Could you change your plans and hurry? I am afraid I am dying. I cannot eat."

"Beth I cannot visit you right now. It will be awhile before I can see you."

Beth started crying and hung up the phone.

Arnold thought of his father. "Always do the right thing," went through his mind. "but what is the right thing here and now?" Arnold asked himself.

For two days Arnold could not get the thought of Beth and what was the right thing to do out of his head. Brenda asked him what was bothering him, and he told her the whole story.

"A hermaphrodite? Hmmm. I'd like to ask a few questions about how that works," Brenda said.

Arnold tried to hide his smile.

"Arnold, get on a flight and go see Beth. I trust you, and you will have done the right thing."

Arnold called the airline and scheduled a flight to Colorado Springs. Then, he called Beth. Beth, I am coming to see you."

"Thank you, Arnold," Beth said sounding stronger already. "I'm in St. Francis Hospital, room 203."

Before leaving home, Arnold told Brenda to call Charlie if she needed anything while he was gone.

When Arnold arrived at the hospital, anxiety flooded over him. He tried to tell himself to get a hold of himself.

"Take a deep breath. This won't be easy, but you can get through it."

He climbed the stairs to the second floor and found Beth's room number. He entered and found Beth asleep. At first glance, she looked thin and small. He went back downstairs to the gift shop and purchased a bouquet of flowers that reminded him of the flowers growing around the place he and Beth had identified as their favorite place on the ranch.

This time when he entered the room, Beth was awake.

"Arnold!" she said. "You did come." She raised her arms and Arnold bent so she could hug him and kiss him.

Arnold felt like he might cry. Beth did not look like herself at all. Her cheeks were hollowed, and her nose, ears, and eyes seemed to protrude. When she smiled her teeth seemed to be too large for her. She was in a terrible state of health.

As he withdrew from her embrace, he noticed her wrist bones stuck out and her arms had lost muscle. She had not yet noticed the bouquet. As Beth reclined back on the pillow, she pled, "Arnold please return to ranch with me and forgive me for all of my mistakes."

Arnold replied, "Beth I love you and I forgive you. That is why I am here. I cannot return to Beth Ranch. I have returned to Oklahoma and I have made my home there. I plan to stay there. I am going to make a new life for myself, and I want you to begin to make a new life for yourself."

Beth said nothing as Arnold paused, but tears streamed down her face and dripped off her chin. She did not bother to wipe them away.

A doctor came in right at that moment and looked at her with concern.

"Miss Houser, I need to take your vital signs again, and I am hoping for some improvement over yesterday's numbers."

Arnold started to get up from his chair. "Do you need for me to leave?" Arnold asked.

"Please stay Arnold," Beth said.

"Okay," Arnold said and sat down waiting for the doctor to finish his work.

The doctor concluded his evaluation and left without saying anything.

Beth asked Arnold, "how long are you going to stay with me?"

"My reservation has an open return date," replied Arnold.

"I hope you stay a long time. I want time to work out our troubles."

"I am willing to discuss anything you want to talk about."

"Do you realize that I have apologized over and over again for the mistakes I have made and that I am sincere about all of it?"

Arnold looked down at his boots and turned his hat in his hands uncomfortably. "At the risk of this conversation taking a negative turn, and you crying again, I have to ask why you and Jerry went to bed together a second time after you said you never would after the first time," Arnold asked.

"Can you believe me if I tell you?" she asked.

"I can try," he promised. "You don't give me much to base my answer on. Tell me Beth."

"It is the same as before, I have not changed. The doctor told me I would always be this way, in other words, not able to say "No" to a man when I am having the sensations I sometimes have. I cannot help it."

"Beth you need to go back to the doctor and have him help you. You cannot go thru life this way. No man will accept you when you show this kind of an inability to say "No" to other men."

"I did talk to the doctor about that. The insurance will not pay for the treatment that I need. It costs twelve thousand dollars."

"Beth get the treatment. Send the bill to me, and I will pay it," Arnold insisted.

Beth smiled and beckoned with her hands to indicate she wanted to hug Arnold. He stood up and leaned over her bed. He kissed her and whispered to her. "Goodbye. I love you and always will, but I have started a new life. You must do the same."

Arnold gave Beth the flowers then. He saw her bury her face in them as he walked out of the room. He returned to the airport and booked a flight home.

While he was waiting for his departure time, Arnold called Shoo Ann.

"Shoo Ann, I have been to see Beth in the hospital, and I am now returning to Oklahoma to resume my new life."

"Arnold, I love you and I will miss you forever. Thanks for visiting Beth," Shoo Ann replied.

"Keep me posted Shoo Ann. You will always be my friend. I will never forget you."

After Arnold arrived home, Brenda wanted to know if Beth was better.

"To be honest, I am not certain. She did say the doctor could treat her and the cost would be twelve thousand dollars. I promised to pay the bill when it is due if she gets the treatment."

Brenda smiled. "It is good that you agreed to help her in that way. Do you love her Arnold?"

"I do love her in the way that Jesus taught us to love each other as brothers and sisters, that being unconditionally. I will probably always love her in that way. I don't want to be directly associated with her because this is my life now. I feel that I can love her and help her without sharing my life with her.

"You are such a good person, Arnold. I guess that is why I married you."

"Would you like a tour my land? — Our land?" Arnold asked.

"Let's go right now," Brenda said.

They got into the truck and began an extensive drive over several sections of land. Arnold pointed out the newest sections he had recently purchased. Arnold told her about Charlie and how they got connected. He told her about Alex and her girls. He drove by the old farmhouse where he used to live as a child.

When they returned to their home, Brenda beckoned Arnold to follow her up the stairs. Soon they were laying close to each other on the king-sized bed. The sun went down. They hardly noticed as the they kissed and made love and talked wrapped in each other's arms.

"This was a great day," Brenda sighed. "I want to keep it in my memory forever. And, making love keeps getting better the more we do it."

"It just takes practice," Arnold. "I'm ready when you are."

CHAPTER 27

"I saw some men working with large equipment off in the distance when we were driving around yesterday," Brenda said as she poured Arnold and herself hot cups of coffee the next morning. "What are they doing?"

"It is an oil or gas well drilling operation. The wells produce several cubic feet of gas or several barrels of oil each month. There are around 30 or 40 on our land. They make enough money for Mr. and Mrs. Barkley to be able to lay in bed every morning and make mad, passionate love till noon if they want to."

Brenda laughed.

As they sipped coffee and ate cinnamon coffee cake, two trucks pulled into their drive. The trucks were cattle trucks. Brenda was pleased when she saw the cattle milling around in them.

"Are they ours?" she asked Arnold.

Arnold was already getting up to go out and talk to the drivers.

"Yes. I believe they are," he replied. "Charlie will be here soon to direct this operation."

"How many cows are there?" Brenda asked.

"I'm not sure. This may not be all of them. I leave that up to Charlie."

A truck pulled up pulling a horse trailer. He stopped behind the big cattle trucks and walked up to Arnold.

"I have a delivery here for Mrs. Barkley," he said.

"Ah good. Beautiful Sunshine has arrived." Arnold said. "Honey come out here. Your pony has arrived too."

Brenda hurried out to the horse trailer, peaking in at the quarter horse mare. Brenda could hardly believe her eyes. The horse was the most beautiful thing she had ever seen.

"Mamm, can you ride?" the delivery man asked.

"I sure can," she replied. The delivery man undid the door at the back of the trailer and led the mare out. Brenda took hold of the rope bridle and much to the surprise of the delivery driver and maybe the horse, though the mare did not move a muscle, Brenda mounted her bareback and rode away from the noisy trucks out into an open field. Brenda let Beautiful Sunshine stretch her legs after the ride in the trailer then returned and dismounted, giving her new pony a hug.

"I am so happy with her. Thank you, Arnold. I guess I'll have to settle with you later."

The truck drivers and delivery man smirked at that. Arnold grinned.

"Brenda, we need to go into town and buy a bridle, blankets, and a saddle for you, plus anything else you want for your quarter horse.

Brenda said, "Let us do that now."

Brenda led Beautiful Sunshine over to the barn and put her into the stall next to Black Shadow. The two horses greeted each other with their noses over the fence between them, then added nips and squeals as the paced back and force looking each other over.

Arnold and Brenda got into the truck and drove to El Reno to purchase tack for Brenda and her horse.

As soon as they got back, Brenda wanted to tour their land on horseback. Arnold agreed."

As they changed out of their "town" clothes back into their working and riding clothes, the phone rang. Arnold answered and it was Beth.

"I am leaving the hospital following the treatment prescribed by mu doctor. I'm feeling much better knowing that I will have some control of myself and my urges from now on. Shoo Ann is coming to pick me up and take me home."

"Good news," Arnold said. "Be sure to send me the bill for your treatment."

"When will I ever see you?" Beth asked.

"I have business in Las Mesitas in a couple of months and will drive over to your place for a visit."

"Okay. I love you Arnold."

"Love you too Beth."

As they rode over the hills and along the fences of their land, Brenda pulled Beautiful Sunshine up to ride close beside Black Shadow. The horses snorted, but well trained as they were, they dared not kick or act up with their riders on board.

Brenda smiled over at Arnold. "I have some news. I have missed my period for a while now and have just found out that I am pregnant."

Arnold took his hat off, stood up in the stirrups, and whooped as loud as he could. Black Shadow pranced around nervously, not sure if that whoop meant there was a lion around or not.

Beautiful Sunshine took a dodge off to the side, but Brenda, on top of things brought her up and around back on track with Black Shadow.

"I guess you are happy too," Beth laughed happily.

Arnold dismounted, ground tied Black Shadow and helped Brenda down out of her saddle. She held onto her reins, not sure if Beautiful Sunshine would run off or not. Arnold wrapped his arm around her still slim waist and bent her over his arm for a long kiss.

"You are beautiful," he murmured and danced her around on the grassy hilltop. Brenda let her horse's reins drop and grasped her hands around Arnold's neck, smiling up at him.

"I need to go shopping again. I need maternity clothes. My tummy is beginning to protrude already."

Arnold took Brenda shopping the next day. He dropped her off at a dress shop that also had a tailor, and while she shopped, he stopped by D, D, & C's offices and told Linda and Darrel about the baby coming. Linda wanted to know the due date and asked if it would be okay if she set up a baby shower. Arnold said he would have to ask Beth about that.

Arnold then stopped by the bank and told Robert and Charlene the news. When he picked Brenda up from shopping, he asked her about the due date and mentioned the shower Linda wanted to throw. They stopped back at the investment office so Brenda could thank Linda for thinking of a shower. She asked her to wait to schedule for two weeks because Brenda had a doctor's appointment, and things would be clearer after that.

At the doctor's appointment, Brenda was surprised by the news that she was having twins. The doctor said everything seemed to be going fine and he clearly heard two strong heart beats in her womb.

Brenda had driven herself this time to the doctor's office, so she called Arnold and asked him to meet her in El Reno for dinner that night. He said he would shower and be there in an hour.

"Well hurry!" Brenda said. "I don't care if you look like a farmer just coming out of the field."

Arnold chuckled, saying, "Well, I care. I'll shower first. See you soon. Maybe you can shop around for baby clothes or something."

Arnold did hurry getting cleaned up because he could not figure out why Brenda would want him to hurry. He already knew about the pregnancy.

Arnold met Beth at the Doctor's office. She motioned for him to join her in her car. She grabbed him in a hug as soon as he got in and said, "How do you like twins?"

Arnold grinned, kissed her, and said, "The more the merrier. I always wanted a family of my own."

They drove their separate cars to a steakhouse and celebrated the good news with steak, potatoes, apple pie, and coffee. Beth hoped the twins were girls. Arnold said he didn't care either way. Beth took Arnold's hand and moved it to her belly.

"I don't know if you can feel two heartbeats, but it does seem like four feet kicking in there. Can you feel them?"

"Yes!" Arnold lied.

He thought 80% of what he felt was his imagination, but he didn't care. They were having fun and Brenda was beaming with happiness. After dinner, walking to their cars hand in hand Arnold said, "What a beautiful happy day."

The next afternoon, Brenda called Linda and told her that the babies were progressing well and that they had 5 months to go until the magic 9th-month delivery date.

"Any time you want to schedule a baby shower is fine and be aware there will be two of them."

"Twins!" Linda laughed. "Too bad we don't know if they are girls or boys. I'll plan the shower for three weeks from today at 2:00 PM."

Brenda and Linda were becoming friends, and they laughed and talked for quite a while before hanging up.

"I am the happiest woman in the world, and Arnold is the happiest man in the world," Beth told Brenda right before they hung up the phone.

Arnold came in the house from feeding the horses. He sat down at the kitchen table and looked at Brenda where she sat on a stool near the phone.

"Are you wondering who to call next with the great news?" He smarted off.

"Mark the calendar for three weeks from today. Linda is scheduling a baby shower at 2:00 for the twins," Brenda laughed.

"I can't help thinking about how far I've come since July 7, 1956," Arnold said seriously. "That was the day I started on this odyssey of a journey. I was the most confused guy in this world. Here it is June 1959, and I am married with a home and babies on the way. Brenda, I hope you will always be by my side for the rest of the trip. Two sweethearts dancing off into the future."

He bowed his head in a silent prayer of thanksgiving. Brenda joined him at the breakfast table and gripped his hands. She whispered, Thank you God.

She heard Arnold say, "Thank you Lord Jesus, my Savior."

After a cup of coffee and a couple of cookies for a snack, Arnold returned to grooming the horses in the barn. He opened he retrieved his brush and gave Black Shadow and Beautiful Sunshine a complete brushing. He checked their ears, legs, and backs for sores or fly bites. He combed out their manes and tails.

After dinner that night, Arnold discussed several business matters with Brenda, including the question of ownership of his ranch in Oklahoma and the ranch she had inherited from her father, Henry, when he died. The ranch was in Colorado. Arnold had rented the ranch on Beth's behalf to Scott Rathmussen for five years. That lease would be up in two years.

"We need to get each other's name on the deeds to the ranches we own now that we are married," Arnold said.

"Now that you mention it, I am anxious to get these business matters done," Brenda said. "What do we need to do?" she asked.

"We will need to go to the recorder of the deeds office here and in Alamosa. I'll have Robert suggest an attorney who can draw up the legal documents for us. A Notary will have to witness our signatures. Do you want to go to Colorado with me and take care of this, or do you prefer that I do it?"

"You know what to do. I think you should go."

"Do you want to sell your ranch if I can get the right amount of money for it?" asked Arnold.

"I would prefer my Dad's ranch be sold," said Brenda. "I don't know though. Maybe we should keep it so each twin has a ranch to inherit."

"There is plenty of land here for the twins to divide up someday. How much money do you want for the ranch if I can get an offer?" Arnold asked.

"Henry told me it was worth $10.00 per acre and there was 2,500 acres. That equals $25,000.00. "

"Will you be happy with that amount?" Arnold asked.

"With the rental price at $4,500.00 a year, I think we should ask for $20.00 per acre or $50,000.00," Brenda said.

"You are a shrewd businesswoman," Arnold laughed. "I agree. Now if someone wants to buy the ranch. Scott might want to buy it. I am prepared with a price."

Arnold and Brenda visited lawyers in Calumet the next week and Arnold scheduled a flight to Pueblo and arranged for a rental car to be available for him there when he landed. He called Beth and informed her he was flying to Pueblo and would call her when he arrived in Alamosa. Beth was pleased and asked where he planned to stay while he was doing business in Alamosa.

I'll stay at Maggie's hotel."

"You can stay here if you would like," Beth offered.

"I don't think I should because I do not trust myself. I am still in love with you and think of you often."

223

Arnold wasn't at all sure why he had not told Beth about marrying Brenda. He felt dishonest acting like he was starting out on a new life all on his own. Heck, he had a wife now and twin babies on the way.

"I understand," Beth said. "Can we meet and talk business?"

"We can do that," Arnold agreed.

Arnold drove out to the ranch Henry had left Brenda right from the airport. He caught Scott Rathmussen as the man was getting ready to leave the house after lunch.

"Arnold Barkley. I remember you," Scott said and shook Arnold's hand.

"Scott. Good to see you again. It looks like things are going well here," Arnold said.

Scott said things were going great.

"Come into the house and have a cup of coffee. I'll write out the rent check for the year," Scott offered.

Over coffee, Arnold broached the subject of Scott purchasing the ranch. "I did come to discuss the rental agreement for the ranch. Brenda and I have married so we are now joint owners. We were wondering if you would consider buying the ranch from us instead of leasing it."

"I would love to if I can afford it," Scott said looking worried.

"We are asking $20.00 per acre."

"That is a fair price," Scott said. "I would love to buy it if you can allow me 10 days to transfer the money."

"Can you pay $5,000.00 today and the balance in ten days?" Arnold asked.

Scott said, "Absolutely," and pulled out his checkbook.

Arnold finished his coffee, pocketed the check, and shook hands with Scott. They agreed to meet in ten days at the Alamosa bank. Arnold drove to Alamosa. He called Beth from the bank where he met with an attorney recommended by the bank manager and invited her to dinner at Maggie's restaurant, suggesting she bring Shoo Ann if she would like to join us.

Beth, Shoo Ann, and Arnold arrived at the restaurant at about the same time, and everyone hugged and kissed, happy to see each other again.

Arnold booked a room at Maggie's hotel for 10 days

After supper, Arnold called Brenda from his room and found out that everything was going well. He told her about the sale and the progress toward making everything legal.

"The attorney here in Alamosa will be sending you a package special delivery. When you get it, take it to Linda. She is a notary and she will help you sign the papers in all the right places as well as witness your signature," Arnold told Brenda. "You should receive these documents in a day or two. Return them as soon as you can. I plan to stay for 10 days to complete the sale of the ranch to Scott. We will need all the paperwork to do that."

"Okay Arnold. I will do all that. I miss you. Take care of yourself. I want you back soon."

"Call me if you need me, Brenda, at this number."

He looked at his room phone and gave her that number as well as the number for the hotel office.

Ten days later, Arnold arrived home in Calumet. Brenda picked him up at the airport. He handed her the checks written by Scott. Now they were both richer in cash and did not have an extra ranch to worry about.

CHAPTER 28

Arnold and Brenda saddled their horses and enjoyed a nice ride through three sections of land. As they rode, they picked out trees to identify. This was not so easy to do now that their leaves had fallen. Beth was quite pregnant by now and Arnold had to help her up onto her horse. They rode at a sedate pace so Brenda could be comfortable. Both riders were bundled up in heavy coats, hats, mittens, and scarfs as the weather had become wintry earlier than normal. It was only November, but a cold invigorating wind blew out of the north.

This was a new and exciting experience for Brenda because where she lived for most of her life was treeless with grass everywhere but trees only in low lying areas where springs provided water to the prairie. Even the names of the trees were interesting to Brenda.

"Well I can identify the Eastern redcedar because it is an evergreen, but what about the Kentucky Coffeetree. I think that is one over there," said Brenda pointing to a tree that was bare of leaves but had a silhouette of mostly large branches and no smaller ones. Large seed pods hung on the tree even though the leaves had fallen.

"Why would a Kentucky Coffeetree, be growing in Oklahoma?" Brenda asked.

Arnold laughed. "I have no idea except that it can. I think my mother used to roast and grind the beans in those pods for a coffee substitute. I guess that is why it is called a coffee tree."

The riders and horses returned to the barn. Both horses were energetic in the cold weather, but something else was motivating Black Shadow as he followed his instincts and Beautiful Summer back to the barn. Being a stallion, he considered it his duty to service any female horse in his company that seemed to be ready to mate. Beautiful Summer was sending him messages of love and indicating she was ready to mate. As they entered the corral, Brenda had to dismount quickly, more quickly than her girth would normally allow because Black Shadow appeared to be ready to mount Beautiful Summer whether Brenda was in the saddle or not.

She had barely vacated the saddle when Black Shadow mounted Beautiful Summer. Arnold quickly moved Brenda out of the way of the horses, steadying her with an arm around her shoulders.

Beautiful Summer had not previously mated and she was unsure about the process. She jumped out from under the stallion. Brenda stood at Arnold's side inside the fence rather close to the two amorous horses, wondering exactly what was going to occur next,

Black Shadow was by now fully erect and ready. He mounted Beautiful Summer and proceeded to perform his duty. Beautiful Summer now seemed ready and stood stock still and accepted the stallion.

Brenda had witnessed horses mating before, but she had never been this close to the action and she had never been pregnant herself, which seemed to add an emotional edge to the situation. The earthy scent of mother nature in action, of stallion, mare, hormones, and the yeasty scent of semen made her head reel a bit. Tears came to her eyes as it hit her that Beautiful Summer was her own horse and she would be receiving the gift of a baby horse in due time.

"How long now until a baby arrives?" asked Arnold.

"About 330-345 days or eleven months," Brenda responded.

"How did you know that?" Arnold asked.

"My father taught me the gestation period of a horse. We had four horses, and when I was little, I wanted a baby colt — now! He pointed out to me that I would have to wait, and I counted every day on my calendar."

Brenda laughed at the memory. She calculated and said out loud, "Eleven months from November will be October. I will mark my calendar like I did when I was a child. Since I am due this month, that means that I will have at least 10 months with my babies before Beautiful Summer's baby arrives. What a blessing."

Arnold unsaddled the horses and hung up the tack, put the mare and stallion in the barn, gave them oats and checked to see they had plenty of water. He closed the gate and followed Brenda into the house. They made love that afternoon with care and once again found themselves eating dinner late after an afternoon of love.

The baby shower Linda organized was an enormous success. All the ladies from the nearby ranches and businesses came. They played games and laughed, ate cake and opened gifts, overall had a joyous time. Brenda was so excited she could hardly remember everyone's name and apologized over and over. She invited everyone to come again when she would be able to better prove her social skills.

"Hopefully, I won't be in such a flurry if you come over for tea some time," she laughed.

Arnold returned the afternoon after the shower from a business trip where he had reviewed his insurance on the farm, added the corral and barn to his property insurance and prepared to add two children to his health and life insurances. Everything seemed to be in order.

He visited D, D, and C and reviewed his investments, adding the proceeds from the sale of Brenda's ranch. D, D, and C said they were staying on top of his investments and would brief him within a week. He reminded them he wanted Brenda to have sufficient time to digest the briefing and they assured Arnold they would see to that. Arnold also reminded them he wanted an income tax quarterly review prior to the April 15 deadline. The consulting firm promised they were in the middle of preparing his briefing with the latest data, including Federal Income taxes.

Arnold listened to the radio after supper that evening. He noticed that Brenda went to bed early. He was glued to the radio because they were forecasting a serious snowstorm would hit Oklahoma sometime the next day. Arnold went to bed late.

At approximately 1:00 AM, Brenda woke Arnold, suggesting they go to the hospital because she thought she might be going into labor. Arnold bundled her up for the cold ride and they left immediately for the El Reno Hospital. Arnold had called ahead, and the hospital was ready for them. They registered in through the emergency room because the hour was so late. Brenda was admitted at 1:45 AM November 12, 1959. Her doctor drove in to examined by her. He requested a cardiologist assist him because he noticed Brenda's heartbeat seemed to be irregular.

Arnold was in the waiting room when a nurse came out to tell him that the heart doctor had ordered an emergency C section removal of the twins. He also ordered that the hospital staff prepare for an emergency heart operation on Brenda.

Arnold sat alone in the waiting room ill with fear. A tortuous hour passed before the two physicians approached Arnold and informed him that Brenda had died during the C section, but the twins, identical baby girls, had survived. Arnold fell to his knees and began to pray. For a long time, he could not do anything but that.

He had not seen his daughters yet. He used the phone in the waiting room to call the Methodist Minister at Red Rock United Methodist Church and ask him to come to the hospital. There was no answer. Arnold noticed his watch and it read 2:00 PM.

Arnold followed a nurse back to the hospital nursery where he met his two new daughters for the first time. He knelt beside their bassinet in the hospital gown and mask they had loaned him. As he looked at the two tiny children, he thought of his own father and mother and wondered how they were able to bear the sadness of losing loved 11 times. He felt sobs rising in his throat and begged God for strength, courage, and health for his new daughters. He sat in the nursery next to his sleeping daughters for hours, leaving only to see Brenda's body before they took it to the morgue and to say goodbye. He sobbed and held her hand, but there was no squeeze in return. She was so still. Her spirit was gone, leaving just her body. He cried for his own loss, and he cried for Brenda. She had been so young, so happy. He cried for his little girls who had no one to feed them and would never know their mother.

After dawn, Arnold was wakened by the nurses coming on to the day shift. They brought him coffee. He had slept in the rocking chair next to the baby girls all night. They were still sleeping in their transparent bassinet when he went down the hall to the bathroom to relieve himself and wash his face. He looked at himself in the mirror and saw a ravaged face bristling with whiskers and puffy from too many hours of tears.

He went to the nurses' station and called Charlie. He told him what happened and asked him to meet him at his house later and he drove home leaving the nurses to bottle feed his baby girls while he changed clothes and fed the animals at the farm.

Charlie arrived at Arnold's house at 8:00 AM. He let himself in and smelled the coffee Arnold had brewed while he took a shower. Arnold was coming out of his and Brenda's bedroom. His face was grey with fatigue and sorrow. Charlie crossed the room to Arnold in a few long strides and hugged his friend who looked so lost in sorrow. He rocked him back and forth as tears came once again. Charlie understood. He knew about sorrow. He was still suffering from the death of his friend and employee Alex. The two friends sat down at the kitchen table and with a notebook in hand, slowly and painfully talked about burial services and cemeteries. Neither had foreseen having to do this again so soon.

Charlie promised to handle all the farm work until Arnold was up to it again so Arnold could concentrate on taking care of his baby girls.

After Charlie left, Arnold faced with the reality of the empty house and a child's bedroom wallpapered with pale green flowers and filled with shower presents. He picked out some little gowns and receiving blankets and warmer blankets for an outer layer. He went back out to the car and headed back into town to the hospital to see when he would be able to bring his babies home. As he drove down the road, he saw Black Shadow and Brenda's horse Beautiful Summer watching the car pull away. Only yesterday, Brenda had exalted over her pregnant mare and counted the days between her own delivery and the birth of a foal. Arnold's loneliness swamped him with a pain that exceeded any he had experienced before.

CHAPTER 29

Arnold brought his twin daughters home in a week. He hired a nanny, who had been recommended by a neighbor to live in, take care of the girls, and cook for them all. Her name was Brook Davis. She was an experienced nanny and a Christian woman who took over the household right away.

Arnold kept thinking that his Lord and Savior was trying to tell him something, but it was not clear in his mind enough to understand what it was. He kept his mind focused on Brenda and their relationship, which he thought was almost perfect, except for the Chaplain. The fact that the Chaplain was back on his mind made him worry about his own sanity. Why should he worry about that now? Brenda was gone. He and Brenda had had a wonderful loving relationship and he did not want to tarnish the memory of it with his jealous fantasies. He kept asking for his Lord to forgive him for not being able to clear his mind of that matter. He asked his Lord and Savior Jesus Christ to guide him and he hoped that would resolve whatever had been bothering him.

Brenda had been buried a week. Every day of that week, Arnold had saddled Black Shadow and rode to the church cemetery where Brenda had been buried. At the cemetery, Arnold walked for hours, around and around through the headstones. Brook took care of the babies.

Charlie told Linda about Arnold walking alone at the cemetery every day, "like a damned ghost" and she visited Arnold at the cemetery during one of his walking tours and she dubbed the exercise, Arnold's, "walking tour of distress." It certainly distressed her to see him like this. She knew he needed time to grieve, but the little girls needed him too and his walking around the cemetery was not giving him any perspective on the future. Linda and Charlie commiserated about what might give Arnold back his confidence.

Linda decided She needed to do something to help Arnold overcome his sorrow and loneliness. She decided to contact Beth. Without consulting Arnold, Linda, who recalled Beth from one of her visits with Arnold prior to his association with Brenda, gave Beth a call.

"Beth, I don't know if you remember me, but I'm Arnold's investment advisor and friend in Oklahoma, Linda," she began.

"I remember you," Beth replied.

"Beth, I don't know if you knew that Arnold had married last year a woman named Brenda."

Beth gasped and then was silent.

"I didn't know. I still love him you know."

"Well, this is awkward, but to hell with it. Let's be straight. Arnold can be an idiot sometimes. I'm calling because Brenda died more than a week ago while giving birth to twin girls. Arnold is sick with sorrow. He has hired a nanny, but he leaves the house every day and walks around the graveyard for hours. The little girls do not even have names yet? For some reason, I thought a visit from you might help."

"Can you hold a minute," Beth asked.

Linda nodded, realizing Beth could not see her. She heard Beth talking to someone else in the background, asking if the other would take her to the airport to catch an airplane to Oklahoma City. Linda felt relieved that Beth was considering the trip and had not just hung up on her.

When Beth returned to the phone, she said she would be there as soon as she could get there but she needed instructions from the airport to Arnold's farm."

Linda said, "Let me know when you plan to arrive and I will pick you up at the baggage claim of the airline on which you are going to arrive."

"That sounds great. There will be two of us. I'm bringing Shoo Ann along."

Linda was relieved. Arnold had told her about Shoo Ann. She thought a little hard- headed Asian pragmatism and wit might be in order.

Beth and Shoo Ann made arrangements to fly immediately to Oklahoma City. The flight was scheduled to depart Pueblo at 6:00 PM that very day and arrive in Oklahoma City at 10:30 PM.

They called Linda and told her. She agreed to pick them up as planned. Linda then called Arnold.

"Arnold, I am bringing a visitor who will be staying with you for a few days. She will arrive late tonight. Can you ask Brook to get a spare room ready?"

"Who is the visitor?" Arnold asked.

"I could tell you, but I want it to be a surprise. Trust me. I know you will approve. You see Arnold, we women have great instincts especially when we joyously conspire to win over a man's heart. That is all I am going to say except, one more thing. Arnold, I have known you for a long time, before your first marriage, your legal issues that gave you such heartache, and before your journey west. I know about your ranch work, your business deals at the bank, your visits with a woman named Beth, and your marriage to Brenda. I am sickened by the death of Brenda. I am heartened though by the birth of your twin girls. I know you will be pleased to welcome your visitor. Please know I do this out of love and respect for you and before you, for your father and mother. I know if your father was here he would challenge you to do the right thing. With that I must go as I have work to do. I will see you later."

After hanging up the phone, Arnold who was in tears again, so sensitive right now that even Linda's good heart made him emotional, walked up stairs and chatted with Brook. Together, they gazed at the twins, taking turns commenting on their beauty. The babies woke up and Arnold took one and Brook the other downstairs where they held them at the kitchen table.

"Are you ready for supper, Arnold?" Brook asked.

"I am somewhat sickened at my stomach. I have no appetite at all," Arnold replied.

"You have to eat Arnold," Brook said as she touched him on the arm. You must eat. You missed breakfast and dinner. Now, it is time to eat and we can discuss what you are going to name these little angels."

They ate supper and discussed appropriate names. They came up with a long list, but no decisions. Arnold nibbled at his meal and as he ate, he could feel his appetite return.

Arnold said, "I think I will ask Charlie and Linda and others to help, but I will make the choice myself after hearing everyone's ideas"

The babies fell asleep and Brook took them back upstairs to their cribs. Arnold noticed the time, and it was approaching 10:00 PM. Before long, a car approached Arnold's house and parked in the driveway. The headlights went out and Arnold opened the front door where he encountered his visitors. There stood Beth, Shoo Ann, and Linda.

Arnold looked at them shocked. His eyes filled with tears. Everyone began to tear up then and they all hugged and wept and smiled. Linda hoped the happiness was a signal that a new life might begin for Arnold. Several minutes passed before Brook came down to see what was going on.

Arnold introduced Brook, explaining she was the nanny to his girls. Brook went upstairs and came down with a sleepy baby in each arm. Beth or Shoo Ann smiled and cooed at the babies and soon had them awake and smiling their big blue baby eyes staring out into space and the arms and feet waving. Brook directed Beth and Shoo Ann places on the couch, and she placed one girl on Beth's lap and one on Shoo Ann's lap and asked each to hold the bottle and allow the little ones to suckle. They both gladly accepted this duty and alternately looked at the little one and cried and looked at the little one and smiled more broadly than ever before.

Arnold watched and was happier than he had been in days. Linda came up behind Arnold, wrapped an arm around him, and asked if he was prepared for the ladies to stay the night.

Arnold responded by giving Linda a hug. "Thank you, my dear friend. Maybe they can stay forever." He smiled and winked.

Linda returned to her home, hopeful that the old Arnold was back.

Arnold sat in the kitchen chair and watched his guests and his babies. He thought of his father and mother and wondered what they were thinking from their lofty position in heaven. He felt himself unwind and relax. Soon, he realized how late it was and offered accommodations to Beth and Shoo Ann. They asked for a brief tour of the house and Arnold was happy obliged to be the guide.

When he came to the spare rooms, he offered Beth and Shoo Ann their choice of rooms. There was no shortage in the house. When they arrived at the nursery, they noticed it was vacant, but when they went into the Nanny's quarter's they noticed bassinets, baby cribs and a double sized bed for the Nanny. Brook came in while they were inspecting the room with the babies and put them into their cribs.

"I just didn't think they were big enough to sleep in the nursery yet," Brook explained. "Here I can hear their every sound."

Once Shoo Ann and Beth had picked the rooms they would sleep in, Arnold decided to retire after a long and tiring day. It had been a good day though. The first one in a while. He crawled into bed and could not sleep. In about an hour Beth crawled into bed with Arnold.

Arnold looked at her and she smiled sadly. "I could not sleep," She said, lying down beside him.

They lay close to each other in silence for a while.

"Why didn't you tell me you married?" Beth asked quietly.

"I didn't want to hurt you. I knew you still loved me, and I still loved you."

"That makes sense. I loved you. You loved me. So, you married Brenda and had twins," Beth said in a straightforward tone as if she was ordering coffee.

Arnold wrapped his arms around her and held her close to him. They laid there recalling times past.

"Let's forget some things," suggested Arnold.

After a couple of hours in each other's arms, Beth asked, "What were we going to forget again?"

"Everything negative," replied Arnold.

"I don't recall anything negative. Can you?"

"Nope."

They went to sleep and dreamed good dreams of a bright and warm future.

CHAPTER 30

Arnold awakened early the next morning and Brook had made coffee the way Arnold liked it, black and strong. Arnold put on his coat as the temperature gage read a minus 10 degrees and he walked to the barn and checked on his two horses. They were standing close together and welcomed him into their circle of warmth with a push of the nose when Arnold brushed them.

He recalled the ranch in Colorado and wondered what was in store for them all when he asked Beth to marry him, which he planned to do that day, maybe before lunch. Whatever occurred, he could handle it.

Arnold returned to the kitchen for breakfast and Brook's great cooking. The twins were in the kitchen with Brook. Beth and Shoo Ann were both still asleep. Brook asked Arnold if he wanted to wait for the two visitors or to proceed without them.

"Brook I want to give you a hug. You have been terrific. There are times when I want to kiss you, but I think you understand that I could not.

Brook stood not looking at him, but at the twins. There were tears in her eyes. She said, "Arnold, I do understand. I am one hundred percent woman, and I understand. I too want to say things to you that are probably inappropriate but in the two weeks I have been here, I have fallen in love with the twins and you. My heart goes out to you and I wish you the best. From what I have heard you say about your parents, about Brenda, about Beth, I have concluded that you are the best man I have ever met, and I was married to a true gentleman for thirty years.

Arnold, I love you like you cannot imagine. I must tell you this to get it off my brain and then we both must go forward. Arnold, I love you and Beth. You are free to release me whenever Beth is ready to take over."

Within a few minutes Beth and Shoo Ann arrived for breakfast. As they gathered around the table Arnold who was drinking hot black coffee asked that Brook sit down with them for a moment. The picture was almost perfect and then it became perfect as Linda arrived and joined them.

Arnold then stood up as if he were going to make a speech and he was. He said, "Welcome to breakfast and please enjoy yourselves as we have a couple of important tasks to complete. One is to review the names we have listed from friends that might be the correct name for each of the twin girls; as part of that task if you have a suggestion to make please add the name to the list. Following breakfast, we will gather in the living room and choose the names of my daughters. So, now let us eat."

"Would you tell us what the second task is?" Linda asked. "We are all interested."

"I am taking a risk with my next task, but I hope Beth will say yes. Beth will you marry me?"

Beth burst into tears and jumped up out of her chair and wrapped her arms around Arnold, giving a huge kiss on the cheek, saying, "Yes!"

She then hugged Linda, Shoo Ann, and Brook one at a time. She proceeded to the bassinets and leaned over the little girls. "It is a pleasure, more than you can imagine, that I have an opportunity I never thought I would have, to kiss my two daughters."

Beth proceeded to kiss each girl on the forehead. "This is more than I would ever ask God to provide to a sinner like myself. I prayed Arnold would become my husband, and I prayed I could someday, somehow become a parent. To have these blessings bestowed on me is truly the act of a very merciful God, and I shall be grateful; Thank you Arnold. And, Linda, thank you for acting on your belief. You are truly a woman of wisdom and faith."

Linda stood and said, "Arnold has been a great guy ever since I met him and before him his parents. I am sure Arnold is doing the right thing."

Everyone ate a hearty breakfast including the twin girls. As soon as the eating was concluded they moved to the living room and began reviewing the list of names. Beth was weepy but managed to collect herself with Shoo Ann's help and reviewed the list adding a couple of her own. As the list was passed from person to person it became obvious that several names were moving toward the top of the list. The total count of suggested names was 74 with seven of the 74 repeats. These seven names were then listed and given to Arnold and Beth to make the final selection. Arnold and Beth moved to the library for privacy and to select two names for each infant. After approximately an hour, Arnold and Beth, returned to the living room and Arnold announced the names of his two daughters as Alexus Ann and Sherry Sue Barkley.

They also announced that they had called the Minister that handled the funeral for Brenda, and Arnold and Beth would become husband and wife the following morning at 10:00 AM, right here at the home of Arnold Barkley.

There was a great round of applause and hugs around with kisses and good well wishes for all. Beth moved to a corner of the kitchen and was talking with Shoo Ann. Arnold stepped up to them and said that he would like for Shoo Ann to relocate to Oklahoma and assist Beth in taking care of Alexus and Sherry.

A grin spread over Shoo Ann's face and she agreed immediately. There was another round of hugs and kisses of happiness.

Brook then stood up.

"Well, I had an ace in my back pocket along. If Beth had refused to marry Arnold, I was going to and I would have adopted the two girls," She said. But, that did not happen. So good-bye to everyone. My work here is finished. I will return home happy, knowing everything that was done was the right thing." She loaded her belongings into her car, and with Beth and Arnold waving to her from the front door of their home, she set out to return to Oklahoma City.

Beth and Arnold stood together with their little girls and thanked God for his blessings.

Following the marriage ceremony, the next day, Arnold and Beth asked Shoo Ann to join them in the kitchen for a discussion regarding the ranch in Colorado. Arnold poured himself coffee. He poured Beth iced tea and poured Shoo Ann a cup of hot tea.

Shoo Ann stood up and said she had a statement she wanted to make first, and Arnold told her to proceed.

Shoo Ann turned to both Arnold and Beth and said, "I am aware of our past life and do not for selfish reasons wish it to end. I have come to know both of you and I want to know from both of you where I fit in as I love you both and do not want to offend either of you."

Simultaneously Arnold and Beth said, "We want you in our lives in the future just as it has been in the past.

"We want no changes," said Beth.

"Except," Arnold added, "We will all live in two places, here and in Colorado."

Shoo Ann's emotions broke out. She hugged and kissed both Arnold and Beth.

Arnold said, "That settled let, us discuss how we are going to handle the ranch in Colorado and the ranch in Calumet, Oklahoma. I see us enjoying one at a time, at times two at a time as some of us are one place and some at the other, and at other times, we will go on vacation."

"Seriously, once the legal stuff was done, I suggest we decide on a schedule based on the functions of each ranch and live in two places. We can manage both ranches with the current staff of hired employees and try to avoid making any long-term decisions for about three years or until they can agree on a better way to live."

"Shoo Ann, you and Beth should sit down and explore your likes and dislikes. We want to make your life as enjoyable as possible, including the economics of it all. You will be included in all private discussions regarding income and expenses, wealth and the future."

Later, Arnold briefed her on his real estate and mineral right holdings including their annual income.

She was shocked.

"I cannot count that high," she said. "Arnold, I knew I loved you but now I know why."

A month passed and Beth asked Shoo Ann to go for a ride on the two quarter horses. Arnold had suggested they do so to help determine if Shoo Ann wanted a horse here as well as in Colorado and the same went for Beth. Shoo Ann said,

"I want my own horse when it is practicable, but I have fallen in love with Beautiful Summer and would be extremely pleased if she were to become my own."

Hearing this, Beth said she would ask Arnold to pick a horse out for her.

"I have already discussed this with Charlie," Arnold said. "You do not need to ask. We are ready to schedule a time when we can go to the Hamilton Quarter horse farm and pick out the horse you like."

"Well then. Is tomorrow too soon?" Beth said sheepishly.

"We will ask," said Arnold.

He called Mr. Hamilton and Hamilton agreed they could come to pick out a quarter horse mare tomorrow at 10:00 AM. He said he would have the ones he recommended ready.

Arnold then called Charlie and asked if he wanted to go along.

Unfortunately, Charlie said he was busy and could not go.

"But, I am not needed," Charlie said. "You can trust Hamilton. Go ahead with good luck."

The appointed time finally arrived, and Beth was almost as excited as a teenager, giggling with happiness. When they arrived at the Hamilton Quarter Horse famr and walked to the corral, Mr, Hamilton had eleven quarter horses Beth could choose from. Mr. Hamilton said they were all of the same blood line and of equal quality.

Beth went right for a young black horse.

"That horse is just like the previous horse I sold you named Beautiful Summer," Mr. Hamilton told Arnold. "The two of them are related. They have papers and cannot be bred by the stallion I own because that is not recommended, but it is perfectly okay for her to be bred by the stallion Mr. Barkley owns named Black Shadow. Both stallions have great blood lines."

Beth was smiling with happiness and told Arnold that the black horse was the one she wanted.

"We need to go to El Reno and have your butt measured for a saddle," Arnold said.

Shoo Ann shrieked with laughter, remembering the first time she was "measured" for a saddle in Alamosa.

On the way to El Reno they kept giggling at Arnold's ornery humor, or at least his attempt at humor.

In the hardware store, Arnold volunteered to do the measuring and that got a good laugh.

"When are they going to deliver my pony, Arnold," Beth asked as they looked at saddles, stirrups, and bridles.

"Mr. Hamilton is getting the papers drawn up and will deliver them within two days."

"When do you think my horse will be old enough to be bred?"

"Black Shadow will let us know. They first to know will be White Beauty."

Arnold snickered, but he was the only one who thought he was joking.

CHAPTER 31

Arnold had a lot on his mind as rode Black Shadow all the way into Calumet. He was going to the bank, but he was preoccupied, thinking about everything he had experienced since that fateful day, July 7, 1956 when drove out of Calumet determined to experience life on the edge without the buffer of money to protect him from life's hardships.

He tied Black Shadow up to a bike rack and walked into the Calumet Bank. He asked to see a bank teller. The most beautiful and thoughtful lady appeared before his eyes. He knew her but it took him a moment to recognize her. To his surprise, the sight of her brought hot tears to his eyes. Sarah, he thought, the love of his life. She smiled a welcomed, called him by name, and asked if she could help him.

Arnold was speechless and stood staring. She was the sweetheart he had said goodbye to a long time ago. Tears dripped from his eyes. He didn't bother to wipe them away. He simply said in a whisper, "Sarah, how are you, I am pleased to see you. Can we go to lunch and talk?"

Linda was nearby or she never would have heard the whispered request, but overhearing, she said, "Sure, Robert will relieve Sarah. Take all the time you need."

Having recovered somewhat from the shock, Arnold found himself standing outside the bank in front of the sweetest woman he had ever known. She was like a saint to him. Arnold felt a little nausea assaulted him when he thought of his own behavior toward her. He wanted to move near Sarah, to hold her, but he merely stood in front of her.

She put her arms around him and kissed him passionately.

She released his lips and beamed up at him. "Welcome home Arnold."

Arnold, now recuperating from the shock of the kiss, thanked her, returned the hug, and kissed her back in a daze.

Trying to remember where he was, Arnold spun around in the parking lot looking for clues to tell him how he got here. He saw Black Shadow tied to the bike rack. He waved his hand in the direction of the stallion and said, "Last year, the Big Guy and I developed a strong relationship. I rode him into town."

Sarah looked at him quizzically. Then she looked at the horse.

He realized he was sounding like a fool and asked, "Can we go to the restaurant?"

"This way, if you remember," said Sarah.

They walked out of the bank and toward the restaurant. Over lunch, they talked of old times. Arnold told her about Brenda, Beth, and the twins. Sarah said she had never married. As they left, he invited her to visit him after she got off work. He remembered that he had left her behind after she had supported him emotionally throughout the whole messy divorce. He was pretty sure she would never visit him, but she promised she would, if she could meet his wife and twin girls.

Sadness filled him as he left her and mounted Black Shadow for the ride back to the farm. At first, he could not think of any reason why meeting Sarah again should make him sad, but it did. It had to do with loss, lost innocence, and lost opportunity to do the right thing, and guilt. He thought of July 7, 1956 and he knew he had hurt her badly, but she had never said a word in complaint.

Arnold detoured back to the cemetery on his way home from town. While Black Shadow grazed, he spent an hour walking and thinking about the miracle of forgiveness.

Life continued to go smoothly for the new little family. Everyone was finding their place in the work that had to be done to keep the farm and home going. During an early morning exercise for the horses, Arnold, Beth, and Charlie were walking the three horses and leading the young mare called White Beauty. Charlie asked where Shoo Ann was, and he was informed that she and Beth had tossed a quarter to see who stayed with the girls, and Shoo Ann won.

"Next time, I will win," Beth said.

"Well, I've been thinking. I'd like a recommendation for someone who can assist me in caring for my cattle and your properties," Charlie said as he rode up beside Arnold and Black shadow.

"Do you think Shoo Ann could do it?" Charlie asked.

Arnold, surprised, responded, "Why yes. She has most of the training. She might need a little more in project management. That is a hell of a good idea Charlie."

"I might talk with Shoo Ann and see if she is interested in performing the work Alex used to do," Charlie said.

"What do you think Beth? She is your friend."

"I think that is a great idea. Shoo Ann needs some work of her own and to get out of the house to meet people," Beth said.

As the three of them returned to the barn, Black Shadow began to demonstrate, as stallions will, his desire to mate with White Beauty who was the only horse to respond his desire. Charlie was leading White Beauty and released the snap on the lead rope from her halter as soon as he figured out what was about to happen. He and Beth quickly moved their mounts ahead of Arnold, out of the way. Arnold, who was riding

Black Shadow, also recognized the signs and did not want to ride the stallion during his favorite activity, mating, in this case with the receptive White Beauty.

Arnold jumped out of the saddle, loosened the cinch, and quickly snatched his saddle and gear off the horse. He carried them into the barn. As he turned around, he noticed Black Shadow mount White Beauty and the entertainment began. Beth watched as the two horses responded to each other just the way Mother Nature planned it. Arnold could not help thinking of Brenda as he reminded himself to mark the calendar for 11 months from now.

"So, Arnold are you as good as Black Shadow?" Beth called over the noisy mating of the horses.

"Always and forever," he responded.

Beth snickered. "Don't I know it."

Charlie pretended not to hear the exchange and walked with Beth and Arnold back to the house as far as his truck. Beth and Arnold waved goodbye as he drove away.

Inside, Shoo Ann and Beth began to get dinner ready. It was comical to watch Beth and Shoo Ann prepare dinner for Alexus and Sherry, and it was even more comical to watch them feed the two girls. Arnold tipped his chair back on its back legs, crossed his fingers over his chest, and watched.

Beth and Shoo Ann comforted each other for their ineptitude by agreeing that they had not performed this function in the past ten years and were surely out of practice, but they were determined to learn and enjoy the experience. Right in the middle of eating, and almost at the same moment, gurgling popping sounds came from each of the twins. Then it was more than sounds. Smells were added, and they each filled their diaper requiring immediate attention.

After the laughter over all the smart comments about the timing, the serious business of changing the diapers began. This was almost as comical as the feeding. But soon everything was quiet, and the two sweethearts were sound asleep without a worry in their heads. Beth enjoyed her two daughters, and this was obvious as she sat next to the bassinets and watched them sleep for a long time.

Arnold walked up behind Beth and hugged her.

"Things are great, aren't they?" he asked.

"Arnold, I love you and I hope we always love each other as we do now," Beth whispered.

Arnold agreed.

"I don't see why anything would ever change."